Go Ahead, Woman. Do Your Worst!
Erotic Tales of Heroes Chained

First Edition

Published by The Nazca Plains Corporation
Las Vegas, Nevada
2007

ISBN: 978-1-934625-43-9

Published by

The Nazca Plains Corporation ®
4640 Paradise Rd, Suite 141
Las Vegas NV 89109-8000

© 2007 by The Nazca Plains Corporation. All rights reserved.
No part of this work may be reproduced or utilized in any form or by any means, electronic or mechanical, including photocopying, microfilm, and recording, or by any information storage and retrieval system, without permission in writing from the publisher. Printed in the United States of America.

PUBLISHER'S NOTE
Go Ahead, Woman. Do Your Worst! is a work of fiction created wholly by *Jasper McCutcheon's* imagination. All characters are fictional and any resemblance to any persons living or deceased is purely by accident. No portion of this book reflects any real person or events.

Cover, Valentin Casarsa
Art Director, Blake Stephens

Dedication

Dedicated to the mighty phallus. When fully loaded, its actions speak louder than words.

Go Ahead, Woman. Do Your Worst!
Erotic Tales of Heroes Chained

First Edition

Jasper McCutcheon

Contents

Triumvirate

Part 1 - The Parade   9
Part 2 – Compare and Contrast   25

Sodium Pentothal Sadists

Part 1 - What's so Funny?   47
Part 2 - Are You a Man?   51
Part 3 - How's My Condition?   55

The Cave Man

Part 1 - Out of the Frying Pan, Into the Fire   59
Part 2 - Corralled   67
Part 3 - Everybody Wants Some Man-Meat   77
Part 4 - Spinning the Wheel   85
Part 5 - Pete Radcliffe: He-man of the West   95

The Boris Bowl

Part 1 - On the Road to Super Sunday	101
Part 2 - Pre-Game Hype	107
Part 3 - Second-half Blowout	119

The Milking Tree

Part 1 - Wrath of the Natashi	129
Part 2 - The Kutambi Elephant	135
Part 3 - The Human Pendulum	141
Part 4 - The Milking Tree	149
Part 5 - Consecration	159
Part 6 - Two Worlds are One	165

About the Author

Jasper McCutcheon	171

Triumvirate
Part 1 — The Parade

"What's all the excitement?"

"They've captured Davidius. Everyone's going to the castle to see him brought before the queen."

The haggard woman dropped her sickle. "Does this mean the end of the revolt?"

"Their army was scattered by a surprise attack last night. Supposedly they were betrayed by a woman in their own camp. Glauken and some of his men escaped, but no one knows to where."

The woman grabbed her daughter's shoulders. "Does Davidius know where they are, Celeas?"

"I'm sure that's what the queen wants to know."

"Then we must go to see it it's true. Glauken is our last hope to end this reign of terror. Davidius must hold out until Glauken's remaining army can attack."

Celeas and her mother left the wheat field where they had toiled all their lives and began the two-mile journey to the village. They arrived just in time to see Davidius being paraded amongst the throngs of people who had come to witness his capture. Displayed inside a metal cage, which sat atop a four-wheeled wooden cart towed by two draft horses, the prisoner's wrists were locked into metal rings attached to a board six inches wide and four feet long. This board ran through metal hooks on the roof of the cage, leaving the man's sandaled feet dangling a few inches from the floor of the cage. As he passed, the townspeople spit at him, threw food both fresh and spoiled at him, all as a way to show their support for the queen. Even those who secretly had backed the revolt now wanted the queen's army to see their loyalty.

"These people change horses easily," the woman said to her daughter.

Nearly in tears, Celeas noticed, "They've removed his shirt, but I see no marks other than what our cowardly friends have hurled upon him."

"They're saving him for her. You know she wets her lips for revenge… and information."

"He'll never tell," blurted the daughter. "He and Glauken have been best of friends since childhood. Davidius will never betray him."

"You, Celeas, have also been his friend since you were children. Try not to think about what might happen to poor Davidius."

The parade ended with Davidius and cart reaching the drawbridge of the castle, where it crossed the moat into an open-air courtyard within the castle walls. As the drawbridge was raised, servants unhitched horses and six of them pulled the cart inside the enclosed court of Queen Miscreantia, whereupon her throne she sat, waiting.

"Present him to me," boomed she.

Two female servants entered the cage and placed metal rings connected by a single chain onto the ankles of Davidius. Other servants disassembled the cage as the two women released the board from its roof, and then Davidius was led off the cart toward her throne. With the board binding his wrists now resting on his shoulders, he stood before his queen.

"So, you thought you could replace me, is that it?" she inquired, her crimson lips matching the crimson trim of her stately, cream colored robe. She sat erect, her spine firmly planted to the tall backing of her carved stone perch, the pedestal upon which it sat elevating her three feet above the floor. "Too bad your lust for women spoiled what little chance you had for success." Her lengthy, dagger-like fingers clutched the vertical edges of armrests, both index fingers impatiently tapping. "But that's all over with now. I only want to know one thing. Where is Glauken?"

Davidius stared directly at her, strained his bound arms and flexed his muscles, but said nothing.

"I expected as much. I have prepared for this day. Balstok come here. How many men have you broken in your career?"

"Countless dozens, your majesty."

"Exactly. You see, slave, I have brought Balstok here all the way from Gaul because of his reputation. I am paying him many pieces of gold to extract the information I need. He will earn his keep by any means necessary because he has no intention of soiling his perfect record. Hopefully, he will start by cleaning you up, since you have spoiled my court with your foul odors."

Davidius still said nothing, but he expanded his chest and sneered at the queen. It was his way of telling all present that he was prepared to suffer whatever tortures awaited him, and that he would not be broken easily.

Balstok and his assistants sprang into action. Grabbing each end of the board, they dragged Davidius to the darkly lit stairwell leading to the bowels of the castle. At the bottom were holding cells and a large room filled with devices used to create pain. Davidius was laid face up on the floor in a corner of the room with the board several inches past his head. Balstok barked, "Strip him," and it was done. "Now clean him. Do not damage any part of his body."

Several of the queen's servants entered with buckets of water, soap and brushes. They drenched the man with water and applied the soap with scrub brushes. One of Balstok's helpers stood on the board to make sure the prisoner would not move, and after he was thoroughly lathered and scrubbed down, the servants retrieved fresh water to rinse away his soap, dirt and odor. Davidius was turned to lie face down for a repeat of the cleaning process before being brought to a standing position and patted dry with clean linens.

His naked victim now clean, Balstok smirked, "Now we can get through this without becoming ill. Unchain his feet and take him to the slab."

The man from Gaul brought his own torture instrument with him, for it was a device he himself had designed and perfected through years of torturing people for confessions or information. Simple it was. A solid block of wood three feet in height, four in width and five in length, its only attachments were a metal wheel with sawed teeth and matching catch-release pin mounted to one end, and two metal rings attached to iron plates bolted to its top surface. The wheel moved the plates, which brought the metal rings with them, and as Davidius was made to sit atop the block of wood these rings were opened and his ankles inserted to them. Balstok closed the rings and locked them shut, while two of his assistants grabbed the board to which the wrists of Davidius were still bound. Pulling back, they forced him to lay face up on the slab, stretching his arms past the other end of the slab before taking the board down towards the floor.

In preparation for their duties as assistants to interrogator, Balstok's men had earlier bolted two cranks to the floor at this end of the slab. Attached to each crank was a chain, which the assistants wrapped around and locked to the board. Now they pulled the board further away from the slab, tightly stretching their prisoner lengthwise, and as the hand cranks were turned, chains pulled the wrists of Davidius down until they were twelve inches from the floor.

The end of the slab stopped at Davidius's shoulder blades. His head hung off the edge of its sharply-cut wood while his arms spread three feet apart in downwardly straight lines from his arm pits to his wrists, all stretched beyond his head. This caused his rib cage to rise high into the air.

Balstok was almost ready to begin his task, but not quite. "Put something over his genitals. I don't want that thing pointing at me all day."

An assistant produced a handkerchief and laid it over the chained man's manly-sized penis and testicles, leaving the rest of his body completely exposed.

And what sort of man lay helplessly chained and awaiting his punishment? What formidable carcass presented itself to challenge Balstok and his henchmen and their dastardly instrument of torture? The ultimate design of masculine strength and beauty, that's what.

From his high-arched and meaty feet with strong tendon lines on top, thick-soled armor beneath, to his massive leg calves lightly carpeted with short brown hairs, their heavy muscles made more dramatic by their flattening to the slab surface; from his big-jointed knee caps to his incredibly-structured thighs covered with slightly longer brown hairs; from the wedge of hair appearing out of his handkerchief loin covering, their swirls forming a thin-lined fur trail on their long path to his belly button, where the knot normally hidden inside an oval now exposed itself, framed by a navel stretched to a slit; from the deep ridge of rock-wall belly muscle running the length between pelvis and stomach, the ridge accentuated and intersected by rippled lines and curves and all horrendously compacted and flattened and stretched, to the end of his sternum where his solid wall of abdomen began its dramatic drop like a cliff; from his mighty rib cage, well-protected by thick muscle, to his heaving, smooth-skinned pectorals, their bulging thickness elevated by the cutting edge of wood beneath his shoulder blades; from his brown-bushed, stretched-wide-open arm pits to his short-cropped brown head hair dangling and inverted, to his nobly-wide but tapered nose, to his focused brown eyes, to his half-melon-shaped biceps and triceps and ballooning forearms and tightly-clenched, hard-as-stone fists, Davidius chained for torture represented everything a man should be: five feet and eleven inches of solid muscle built naturally from hard labor and lightly painted with manly fur in all the right places.

What he would be when Balstok and his henchman were finished with him was anyone's guess.

Balstok sat on a stool in front of his prisoner's inverted face for a bit of taunting. "Here you have no name. To me you are nothing but a slave and I will address you accordingly. I call this device the slab as a nickname, but officially it is known as my back-breaker stretch rack."

Davidius flexed his chest and tried to raise his arms, testing the strength of the torture device.

"I know you can't see, but those rings holding your feet are adjustable. I can turn a wheel and move them toward either end of the slab. Then at this end, your crucifixion board can now be raised or lowered as I please. I've added little additional procedures that we can apply while you are stretched here. There's only one way for you to avoid all this and that is to tell me the whereabouts of this man named Glauken. Do you want to tell me now or will I need to persuade you?"

Davidius already struggled to breathe. Being stretched like this compressed his diaphragm so that his stomach could hardly rise to receive air, but still, he gasped for short, quick intakes, glared at his tormentor and grunted with defiance, "Do what you must."

"Start with the 20 blows!" boomed Balstok, and two henchman approached the slab, each carrying a leather strap two inches in width. Davidius lifted his head to watch them take their positions on either side of the slab. Allowing his head to fall back, he smiled at the interrogator still sitting on his stool. Balstok smiled in return and gave the order, "Whip him."

The men began alternating blows with the straps, each one striking across the man's mighty chest. Davidius's arms bulged as he struggled against the board stretching him. This made his chest expand even bigger, further elevating as it received the blows, one from his left, one from his right.

"Cover the entire chest," barked Balstok. The straps came down on Davidius with accuracy, striking from the armpits to the end of his rib cage. One struck his sternum, another across his nipples. The leather was too wide to draw blood, but heavy red lines soon began to form upon his skin. With each man reaching his own count of ten blows, the whipping stopped.

"Where is your friend?"

The eyelids of Davidius were clenched shut as he relaxed his arms and chest. Balstok raised a finger and pointed towards the victim's feet. One of his assistants turned the wheel and the ankle locks moved toward the end of the slab, further stretching the victim's length, bringing from him a slight murmur. Satisfied with the new tension placed upon his racked man's powerful body, Balstok raised his hand and the wheel was locked.

"You have only begun to feel the power of my beautiful invention, slave. Now tell me, where is Glauken?"

Davidius opened his eyes but said nothing.

"20 more blows." and the whipping of his chest resumed. Ten from each side creating more marks before it stopped. "Are you ready to talk? Where is Glauken hiding?" There was no answer. "You gambled and you lost. There is no one here to help you now. You are the only man who can stop this. You must talk."

Now the chest of Davidius heaved at a rapid pace, as he tried to regain oxygen and recover from the second round of whippings. With one mighty gulp of air he blurted, "None of your tortures will break me."

Balstok laughed. "We shall see about that." He turned the cranks on either side of his stool and the chains pulled his victim's arms one inch closer to the floor. As it did the back of Davidius arched to a worse degree, his chest protruded further upwards in a horrific, yet glorious expansion and stretching. The only parts of Davidius's body now touching the slab were his heels, calves and shoulder blades, and he groaned and gasped for air as his unholy suffering intensified.

Balstok sneered, "Feel better, slave?" Turning to an assistant he pointed to the stairwell. "Tell Brutheim I'm ready for him."

The inverted eyes of Davidius blinked. Was the behemoth making its way down each step man or beast? With thick black hair covering every inch of white-as-snow skin, the mass moved ape-like, its hulking chest and arms caveman-like. It was completely nude. Its menacing phallus swung side to side in unison with its gait, pre-come dribbling from the slit of this club-like appendage, and Davidius shuddered when he saw what rested upon this Brutheim's shoulder: another club, very real and very much made of wood. Rounded at one end where it was three inches thick, the club tapered its four-foot length to a one-inch point.

The thing approached and joined its master, Balstok, in standing near the crucifixion board so that Davidius could clearly view the upside-down image of both.

"This man is not yet ready to talk, Brutheim, so I will turn him over to you. Perhaps you can persuade him. I believe it is time for the 10 blows."

The beast was human. It answered, "Yes, sir," and proceeded to scan with his eyes the helpless victim's terribly stretched body. It stalked around the slab scrutinizing every inch of this masculine form as though Davidius was quarry given to him for the hunt, for dispatch, for annihilation. Target chosen, it stopped and licked its lips while Davidius lifted his head best he could to see what was happening. Brutheim stood with club resting on shoulder, his eyes frozen greedily to one particular place. With spittle drooling from the corners of his mouth, the beast reached down with free hand and dug his thick fingers into tightly stretched belly muscle. He manipulated the abdominals on either side of the man's navel as though they were a mass of bread dough. Davidius dropped his head and whispered to himself, "Oh, my god."

Brutheim raised his club high into the air and brought it down full bore onto the victim's belly. Another blow immediately followed the first, and Davidius tightened his stone wall with all his strength. Each pounding of wood to muscle brought masculine grunts and groans of "oomph" and "hooagh," along with deep-toned thuds of penetrating club against unyielding strength. The horrific impact caused the flimsy handkerchief to fall between tensed thighs and down to the slab, leaving Davidius completely naked as he withstood this ungodly beating. Masterful in his accuracy, the beast pinpointed each pounding of the club strictly to muscle, working the entire surface of lower belly from navel to just above the pelvic bone until ten blows were given.

Round one was ended, but Balstok gave his prisoner no time for recuperation. Leaping onto the slab, he planted both knees atop his victim's mighty chest, grabbed Davidius with both hands clutching his head and violently jerked upwards, bringing them face to face. "Where is Glauken? Give him up now!"

"No," Davidius gasped, his teeth clenched and lower jaw extended. "Never."

Brutheim joined Balstok on the slab and stood over the victim's belly. Reversing grip on his club, he placed the small pointed end just below the navel of Davidius, leaned on it with his entire weight and ground its tip into tortured muscle. The feet of Davidius writhed. His toes curled. A long, deep-throated grunt accompanied his straining and flexing attempt to withstand the impalement of Brutheim's club, as he raised his chest and sucked in his belly with all his might.

"Why don't you talk? Your friend would have given you up long ago. Where is he now?"

Words could not penetrate fog. Davidius focused all thoughts to the stake, all defenses to his tortured belly. The force of Brutheim's impaling club sent shockwaves from the depths of his bowels to the skin of his nuts to the tips of his toes, but his powerful muscle held wooden spear at bay.

"You will talk, damn you. Do you think this is the worst I can do?" Balstok released his prisoner's head and leapt from the slab, while Brutheim continued grinding the club into muscle. "Brutheim, come here and use your other club on him."

Removing the stake, Brutheim tossed it to the floor and followed it there, moving to join Balstok near the inverted face of an agonized man. Davidius repulsed the urge to puke. The sounds he made mirrored his attempts, as he gallantly struggled for oxygen with rapid breaths, his expanded chest and flattened belly rising and falling at a frantic pace. With his eyelids shut tight, he did not see his two antagonists standing so near him, did not expect the smack of skin across his cheek. His eyes opened just in time to see the second whack coming, but it was no hand slapping him. No, what Davidius saw was the grotesquely plump and slimy cock of the beast named Brutheim. Its massive girth taunted him; its nasty ooze smeared him; the degradation he felt enraged him.

With laughter from Balstok and Brutheim adding to his humiliation, Davidius violently attempted to snatch the offending organ in his chomping teeth. Brutheim stepped back, looked to Balstok for assistance.

"Here, I'll put a stop to that," sneered the sadistic Balstok. He clutched with both hands the hair of Davidius and immobilized the pitiful man's head, forcing him to endure this outrage. As Brutheim resumed slapping the prisoner with his massive tool, each blow caused arousal: more length, more width, and more pre-orgasmic syrup. Davidius shut his eyes, pursed his lips. He suffered what no man should suffer while hoping and praying that none of this animal's fluids entered his turned up nostrils.

"Talk, slave," Balstok barked. "Talk now and I'll make him stop."

Davidius now had two reasons not to answer. He dared not open his mouth.

"20 blows!"

The leather straps once more rained down onto the chest of Davidius. He groaned through tightly-closed lips with each blow to his reddened skin, while Brutheim's fully-hardened meat continued to slap and slime him.

"Where is Glauken? Where is he hiding? Talk, damn you."

As the leather straps neared the end of a 20 count, Davidius felt a warm, gooey liquid strike his inverted face. It was what he'd feared. The hideous pervert had masturbated on him. His nasty sperm landed on the victim's mouth, nose and cheeks. Davidius shot air out of his nose and mouth, trying to blow away the offending mass of beastly semen, as Balstok released his head and both antagonists stepped back. Both laughed and ridiculed their hapless victim.

"You goddamned sons of whores!" Davidius violently shook his head side to side in an attempt to fling off the sticky goo. "You'd best kill me before leaving this land." He fought tears of anger, overwhelmed by this ultimate of degradations inflicted upon him. "Because I will hunt you down and kill *you* first chance I get."

Balstok continued to mock the man. "You will not get that chance. But you will soon wish you were dead if you don't tell me about Glauken."

"Go to hell!"

Balstok turned the floor cranks and lowered his victim's arms another inch. Now with his spine nearly broken in two, Davidius howled in unholy agony. His heels touched the slab. His shoulder blades were cut by its edge. All the rest of his tortured body rose towards the ceiling, his chest and tits the top of a dome, his abdomen nearly separating from his rib cage. So flat was his belly and compressed was his diaphragm that none but miniscule amounts of oxygen could be brought to his lungs. Only a man with the strength of Davidius could have breathed any of it, and even so, only non-stop, dog-like panting kept him alive.

Motioning to Brutheim, Balstok pointed to the slab. Dribbling post orgasm ooze as he swaggered back to the center of the slab, Brutheim swung his wooden club in a full circle and brought it down with a devastating blow to the belly. The hapless man grunted in agony as the club rained down on his powerful muscles again and again. Balstok grabbed him by the throat and demanded, "Talk. Talk now, damn you!"

As the tenth blow pulverized the man's belly, Queen Miscreantia and her entourage of six female attendants and four male guards descended the stairs. Balstok ordered all torture stopped as he and his men stood in deference to her.

She looked and listened. She saw Davidius horrendously stretched and heard the groaning and gasping of a tortured man. Circling the slab to inspect the heaving chest and belly of her prisoner, this gloriously defiant man, his powerful muscles flexed to capacity, their skin covering bathed in manly sweat from his heroic efforts of resistance, she reached down with finger and scooped a sample of his liquid from out of his navel. She licked her finger. She tasted the man, tasted his suffering, tasted his incredible strength, and she fought the temptation to admire Davidius, to pity him, to fling herself atop his tortured body and comfort him, beg him to give in, plead with him to tell his story true or false just so he would suffer no more.

But that would defeat her purpose. After all, the man whose whereabouts she needed to know fully intended to kill her. The man stretched before her would do the same if given the chance, and so with a return to reality, a suppression of the tingling between her legs and a renewed purpose to extract necessary information, the queen composed herself and reassumed her superiority.

"I finally heard screaming, Balstok. Has he talked?"

"No, your majesty."

"Well, ask him again."

Balstok grabbed one of the leather straps and struck the chest of Davidius. "Where is Glauken?" Brutheim jumped onto the slab. He stood with both feet in the pit of the victim's stomach and ground the pointed club directly into his stretched navel. Balstok whipped the chest three more times. "Where is he hiding?"

Davidius raised his head and looked over his tortured chest at Balstok. His face was clenched as he summoned every ounce of strength to withstand the punishment. He could see Brutheim's hairy buttocks above him as the tip of the club was driven like a stake into his navel. He was suffocating from the weight of the hulk standing on his stomach. After one quick glare of hatred to his queen, his arch enemy, the perpetrator of all that had and was now happening to him, Davidius smiled at her. Despite his horrific struggle: back arched and body stretched on the back-breaking stretch rack, chest brutally pummeled with leather, belly ruthlessly impaled with blunted point of wood, compressed diaphragm further restricted by the weighted hulk of beastly man, Davidius thrust out his lower jaw, bared his teeth to his queen with a sarcastically defiant grin, and then dropped his head, let out a mighty groan and shut his eyes to concentrate on his task of survival.

"That's enough!" shouted the queen. As the torture was stopped, Davidius' body collapsed in exhaustion, and even though his muscles no longer fought the leather whip and wooden club, they remained horrifically stretched and glistening with sweat. They still were needed for the difficult task of sucking air into his lungs. Great effort still was required just to oxygenate his bloodstream which in turn would replenish strength to his overworked muscles.

Again she stalked him for inspection, not knowing which angle she preferred. From the crucifixion board she could admire his anguished and inverted face, sweat matting the hair of his head and dripping to the floor.

She could absorb his open arm pits, their thick bushes matted in wetness as though drenched with buckets of water. From the side she could gasp at the sight of his powerful chest, the edge of slab supporting his torturously curved spine and causing his pectorals and man-tits to reach for the ceiling. Here, too, could she gaze upon his flattened abdominal wall, its dramatic drop from his sternum making it appear almost as a separate entity, an entity protected only with muscle and no bone. She was faltering. Her prisoner's masculine physique bedazzled her far beyond any man who'd ever before displayed himself in her chamber of tortures, but still she was not ready to surrender. Balstok's services did not come cheaply, and she endeavored to give him one more chance. She also lusted to see the mighty Davidius once again fight him.

The queen waved Balstok to the far end of the room for a private conversation. "You're taking more time than I anticipated, Balstok."

"Your highness, I've never seen any man withstand torture such as this. How much more can this man take?"

"How should I know? This is your area of expertise, not mine. I've paid you well and I expect results soon."

"He will be broken. Soon."

Balstok stormed toward the slab barking orders. "Turn the wheel." Davidius' feet moved closer to the end of the slab, stretching him tighter. "Turn those cranks." His arms inched closer to the floor, causing Davidius to howl in agony as his back and chest arched beyond the tolerance of any normal man. "Give him the 20 plus 10!"

Leather straps came down upon his chest. Wooden club pulverized his belly, as Balstok crouched in front of his victim's anguished face to interrogate. "Where is Glauken? Give him up now."

Sweat flew from the tortured body of Davidius as his chest was whipped and abdomen pummeled. He shook his head side to side.

"No...Never...NO."

As each count reached the halfway mark, Balstok grabbed the man's hair and shook his head. "Where is Glauken? Talk now. Where is he hiding?"

A complete collapse interrupted the counts of leather and club. The resistance of Davidius was no more. His brain shut down to protect itself, abandoning his body to fend for itself. Mercy was granted Davidius. Unconscious, his brain took him far away from the agony of his tortures.

Realizing that Davidius was not responding, Balstok quickly ordered all beatings to stop. The only movement came from a rapid rise and fall of his mighty chest and belly. The only sounds came from his gasping breath.

"You fool!" boomed the queen. "You are going to kill him. Look at his amazing strength. Don't you see that you'll never break him that way? Apparently where you come from the men are physical weaklings and break down easily. The subjects in my realm are strong of body, but weak in mind. You have failed me, Balstok. I am losing my patience with this. Release this man from his chains and stop this torture. I will deal with him myself."

The queen motioned for her servants to remove the limp body of Davidius from the slab after Balstok's men unchained him, while loud pops and snaps of vertebrae accompanied the release of Davidius from his unholy, back-breaking stretch rack.

"Fortunate for you this man did not die here today, Balstok. Then I would have had *you* tortured on that hideous device. I will pay you in full, and then you and your men can get out. Your slab stays here. It is your gift to me for your failure - and your expression of gratitude to me for allowing you to leave this dungeon alive."

Davidius, still unconscious, was carried by the queen's guard from the slab to a wooden plank for transport, and they stood with him elevated between them awaiting further instructions. Naked upon his plank he laid with arms outstretched, his skin still glistening with sweat, his brain still peacefully absent. She gazed upon him. She relished his beauty, admired his strength, shuddered at the thought of herself undergoing and withstanding the punishments he had suffered. She secretly planned his distant future while verbally expressing his immediate.

"Take him to a cell and revive him. I want him well-fed and pampered. Attend to the wounds on his chest and massage his belly back to health. Bathe and moisturize his skin with salves. I want the marks on his body healed."

And so it was done. Two of the queen's guard transported Davidius up the stairs, while the other two stood watch for her transfer of coin from her purse to Balstok's hands.

"Now, get out!" and the two guards escorted Balstok and his three henchmen out of the dungeon, out of the castle, to the stables and onto their horses. The two rode with them all the way to the edge of their queen's lands, watching and waiting for them to disappear over the horizon.

That evening Davidius was given loving tenderness. Many of the female servants had witnessed his suffering and were grateful that they were gifted the duty of caring for him.

It seems that Queen Miscreantia was taking pity on Davidius, and her show of mercy to a prisoner so dangerous was indeed a rarity. He troubled her, but he also impressed her. A self-induced torture consumed her evening, for this queen found it very difficult to contain her excitement over what she had planned for the next day's activities.

Part 2 – Compare and Contrast

The sun never shines in the depths of a castle. Davidius was awakened by the sound of keys unlocking his cell door. Two of the four female servants who'd tended to him all night were the first to enter. He remembered during his heavy slumber their gentle hands bathing, massaging and caressing his skin, cradling his head, healing him with calming salves, squeezing tensions out of his knotted muscles. They had done everything the queen ordered them to do. Although his chest was tender when touched, the red marks were but a faint pink. His abdominals were sore, but it was a good pain, the kind familiar to him as a result of strengthening crunches, an exercise he performed daily. Both the spirit and physicality of Davidius were rejuvenated, and now two female servants presented him with a lavish breakfast, his second meal since being unchained from his place of torture.

As Davidius accepted his breakfast tray, he was elated to see that one of the servers was his old friend Celeas. He looked at her with recognition, but said nothing, and after Celeas smiled and knelt with him on the floor, Davidius asked the other servant if he could speak with her alone while he ate. She agreed. She left Celeas and Davidius to private conversation, locking the door with her exit.

"Celeas, what are you doing here?" He looked at her with consternation, as he knew there was only one way for a woman to obtain work inside the castle. She had to offer herself to the queen's guards and any who wanted to have her could do so, starting with the highest rank on down. It was a form of initiation, a test of loyalty to the queen, and a pretty woman like Celeas most likely would have had to service several men on her first night. "How could you do this to yourself?"

"Listen carefully, Davidius," she softly spoke. "I had to do it for you and Glauken… and the revolt. He is coming for you. I have found for him a secret entrance to the castle which will lead them down a hallway to the dungeon itself. Word has been sent."

"So you know where he is?"

"Yes. I spoke to him while you were being tortured. I remembered a special place the three of us used to go when we were children."

"The place I will never tell."

She nodded in confirmation. "The only way I could get Glauken the information he needs in order to find you was to become a servant here. So last night I did what I had to do. Most of the queen's army is in the countryside looking for him, so once he gets here he should face little resistance."

Davidius kissed her on the cheek. "You have sacrificed a great deal, little Celeas."

"I gave instructions to my mother. She is taking the message to him now. I don't know what the queen has planned for you today, but you can remain strong knowing that Glauken will soon be here."

"I think Queen Miscreantia is fond of me. If not for her, I would be dead now. The torture I endured was even more than she could bear to watch."

"I know you suffered. The other servants told me what they did to you. You must be strong, Davidius. We will attack them from the inside."

Davidius finished his breakfast and Celeas summoned the guard to let her out of the cell, but before the door could be closed the queen and two guards entered.

"Stand up, my prisoner."

Davidius rose to his feet and stood naked before his queen.

"Thank goodness you look like a human being again. That maniac Balstok nearly killed you. He never told me part of his process was to beat you so. I believed you would only be stretched."

"Am I supposed to forgive you now?"

"I expect you to show me some respect. I am your queen whether you like it or not… and I did save your life."

"None of it would have happened if not for you."

"No, Davidius, that's where you are wrong. It was a woman who put you here. Have you forgotten how you were betrayed? Had you shown a little more discipline you would never have been captured in the first place."

"You're saying I should never trust anyone. Why should I trust you?"

"I'm not asking you to. I want you to tell me where Glauken is so we can all three talk of compromise."

"There's nothing to say. You have oppressed our people long enough and you will pay for it."

"Then we must return to the dungeon. Guards, take him away."

Four men entered the cell, one of them carrying Davidius' crucifixion board from the previous day. With fists flying he fought them. Davidius managed to throw one of them against the cell wall, but the two guards already there joined the fray, making it five against one. Soon Davidius was subdued, his arms stretched and wrists chained to the board.

Two of them lifted the board and carried him to the dungeon with his feet trailing, held aloft by two other guards. The trip was agonizing for Davidius. Gravity forced his back to arch once more as he was carried with his chest and belly facing the floor, his penis dangling below him. Each step of descent racked his body with jolts of pain, as the guards made their way to the dungeon. Once there they held the board while two guards secured it with chains hanging from the ceiling. Underneath, metal rings with chains attached to the floor were clamped onto his ankles before the crucifixion board was raised higher. Vertically suspended six inches above the floor with his arms and legs spread far apart, the naked torso of Davidius formed a midair X shape, as Queen Miscreantia approached with an observation.

"Oh, look, he got his feet dirty. They must be washed."

Female servants performed the task and the queen was pleased with their work. "Now Davidius, you will find my methods are vastly different from those used on you yesterday, but by the time I am finished with you, you will gladly tell me the whereabouts of your friend. You could tell me now, but I am rather looking forward to what I have planned for you."

"You will soon be dead, my dear lady."

"Not by your hand. You are not in a position to make threats. Think back two nights ago. Do you remember what you were doing? You were sewing the seeds of your downfall." Queen Miscreantia turned to one of her guards. "Fetch her!"

Down the stairs came a woman, a naked woman escorted in a not gentle way by two guards. He knew this woman, her name Lyzelma. He had slept with her, trusted her, and she is the woman who told the location of their camp.

"Let me go, you bastards!" she screamed. Kicking and squirming herself free from the clutches of her escorts, Lyzelma ran to the crucified Davidius. She kissed what she could reach: his belly, wrapping her arms around the small of his back to frantically peck and plead.

"Oh, Davidius, please forgive me. They told me you would not be harmed. They gave me enough money so we could live free forever under the queen's protection. I did it for us. None of this was supposed to happen. They tricked me."

She continued kissing his middle section with explanations in between. "They forced me to watch yesterday. I was bound and gagged in that cell right over there. I wanted to cry out to you. I wanted to help you through your suffering. Watching your torture was like torture for me, too."

Queen Miscreantia closely watched the spectacle, paying particular attention to the flaccid penis of Davidius. Did he still have feelings for this fallen woman? Would her touch still arouse him? The queen soon had her answers.

"Get away from me, you cow!" Davidius swung his belly forward to cast Lyzelma aside. "You are a fool. Did you really think you could trust this woman? A tyrant who has forced us to toil like slaves all our lives? What did you think was the purpose of our fight?"

"Please, please, my love. You must believe me. I wanted us to be together forever. I was blinded by my love for you. I wanted what was best for us. You must forgive me, Davidius."

"Love? I never loved you. You were nothing but a come pot to me. As long as your pussy was tight, I'd take it. Once I had it stretched, that was to be the end of you."

Lyzelma fell to the floor, sobbing, and just the same as yesterday, Queen Miscreantia confronted two emotions: she was disappointed that Davidius had not been aroused, thus denying her a view of his hard cock, but she was pleased that his attitude towards this woman had turned cold and vengeful. The queen sought to warm Davidius to her a bit by punishing the woman who'd caused him so much suffering.

"Let's teach her a lesson for being so foolish. Take her to the cross."

The Saint Andrew's cross stood upright directly across the room from the suspended Davidius. Broken-hearted and still-crying, Lyzelma was bound to the leather straps on the cross and left hanging, stretched in an "X" shape just like her ex-lover, and as if crucifixion weren't punishment enough, this cross had a rather unique feature awaiting her: centered to its back side was an axle, and attached to the axle was a handle which when turned caused the cross to spin with its victim taken along for the ride.

The queen stayed close to her male prisoner, the only one of interest to her. "This should give you some satisfaction, Davidius… seeing her suffer the way she made you suffer. Now watch."

She nodded and one of her guards turned the handle. Lyzelma's journey to nowhere began, and as it did another guard stood in front of her with a thin rawhide whip. He ruthlessly laid its leather to her naked skin. The whip could strike her at any given spot as she was spun in a clockwise motion. She screamed with each lashing, with each cut, as the whip brutally sliced her legs, her face, her stomach and her breasts. Spinning white became spinning red. High-pitched shrieks echoed throughout the torture chamber, and while Davidius watched the pitiful woman being cut to shreds, Queen Miscreantia kept a close eye on his manly cock. There was movement, just a hint of growth.

This please his queen. She ordered the spinning to be halted so that Davidius could see the end result. From face to feet, bloody red lines painted delicate flesh, and the head of Lyzelma fell back between her shoulder blades as sobs and moans oozed from her throat.

"Invert her," chirped the queen. One half revolution of the cross suspended the bound woman upside down. "You boys play nice and take turns. Go by rank."

One of them approached the cross and buried his face into Lyzelma's spread-wide-open vagina. While he licked on her, another four guards removed their clothing and assaulted her defenseless body. Male spit replaced female blood. Tits were licked. Nipples were licked. Arms, belly, legs and feet were licked. Foreplay progressed to invasion, as one stepped up on a pedestal and plowed his cock into her anus. Another grabbed a wooden pole, rammed it into her pussy hole. A crucified woman screamed. She contorted and squirmed, as five merciless brutes attacked her, invaded her, and rendered her a useless rag.

"Don't you wish you could join them?" asked the queen.

"You disgust me. Why don't you let her go? Haven't you punished her enough? She can't help it if she's stupid."

Pleased with herself, the queen teased her male prisoner. "I noticed your penis stirring a bit as you were watching her punishment." She placed her fingertips beneath the balls of Davidius, scratching him lightly. "Are you getting some satisfaction from this?"

"Don't concern yourself with my penis. It does what I tell it to do."

"Really!" the queen laughed. "That sounds like a challenge." She scanned up and down the man's powerful form, fixing her eyes on his cock, its beginning arousal causing a protruding-forward separation of penis from nuts. "You better tell it to calm down."

She turned to the men attacking the helpless Lyzelma. "I need four of you over here." The naked guards came to her and she pointed to her prisoner's cock. "Put a harness on that thing. I think it might get out of control."

One of the men took from the queen a leather ring one-half inch wide and worked it down to the base of Davidius's half-erect penis. Attached to the bottom of the ring were three serpentine chains, each seven inches long.

Davidius shuddered. "What the hell are you doing? Whatever you have in mind, it won't work."

She grinned, not bothering to hide her cruel lust for what she had in mind to do with him. "Davidius, I regret to inform you that I must return you to the slab. I've modified a few things that should make it a little more bearable for you. Of course, you could tell me where Glauken is and I might alter my plans."

"You are sick. You are more devious than I ever imagined. I will never tell you what you want to know."

"Good. I'm glad you are ready to fight me." She grabbed hold her prisoner's quickly-inflating phallus and gave a light squeeze. "Take him."

The four guards released his ankle locks and unchained the crucifixion board. They carried Davidius back to the slab, once again securing his feet before laying him atop its surface, but this time his board was removed. Instead, his wrists were locked by metal rings which were attached to chains leading to the floor cranks. Davidius was allowed to bend off the end of the slab naturally and the chains were tightened to secure him there. Although he was not stretched as tightly lengthwise, Davidius groaned as the pain from yesterday was revisited. The edge of the slab dug into his shoulder blades and his chest rose into the air. His elbows were bent at 45-degree angles while his wrists were parallel with his head. Again his face was inverted, this time dangling nine inches below the edge of the slab.

Suddenly Davidius felt his penis being manipulated and he looked up to watch. One of the guards was attaching the chains from his cock ring to little hooks screwed into the slab. Standing straight up and kept fully erect by the cock ring, the mighty phallus of Davidius pointed directly to the ceiling, a handsome attachment of two-inch diameter rising nearly eight inches from his ball sac. This, thought the queen, was a manly tool befitting the manly man to whom it belonged.

A horrific scream pierced the air and Davidius dropped his head. Lyzelma was the source, her shrieks caused by the guards who'd turned her upright and were taking turns with simultaneous fucks to her pussy and her ass. All blood had been licked from her tortured skin, but her anguish had only begun. Davidius realized that he, too, was locked in the chains of a madwoman, and he wondered what sorts of violations were planned for him.

A sitting chair had been brought into the torture chamber, ordered by the queen for her viewing pleasure. It sat upon a pedestal positioned near one corner of the slab, a short distance from her prisoner's stretched arm pit. From here, she could observe proceedings from above, and as her bound muscle-man strained against his chains, with his erect cock held vertical and full of blood by its leather ring and mounted-to-slab attachments, she launched her own form of torments.

"I think our prisoner is ready to begin. Bring in my experts."

Davidius jolted as six naked females descended the stairs. He remembered how Brutheim's penis had menacingly swung from side to side, and now he was confronted by twelve bulbous breasts doing the same. Each female stirred him with their beauty. Their skin appeared soft and supple, their length of hair flowing freely to the middles of their backs with all colors represented: blonde, brunette, red and black. Eyes were green, blue and brown; lips were pink and red, full and voluptuous, and Davidius would desire any or all of them in a soft fluffy bed. But here? Like this? Chained and helpless? Davidius confronted an unknown mix of emotions from dread to lust, and with no clue as to whether they were here to love him or to hurt him, with no ability to do anything about it either way, he lowered his head and closed his eyes, waiting and wondering what atrocities the queen had in mind.

Six feminine beauties approached the slab and stopped, three standing on either side a naked, erect and vulnerable man.

The queen pointed to one of her female assistants and she knelt on the slab next to his chest. Bending forward, she flicked the tip of her tongue against the tip of his left nipple.

"What are you doing to me?" he asked, lifting his head to see her forefinger lightly scrape the tip of his tit. He flexed his arms and chest in a vain attempt to get at his tormentor.

Queen Miscreantia rose from her chair and slowly strolled to the end of the slab between the arms of Davidius. "These women are professionals. They each have been assigned a particular body part. Together, we will make you feel things you have never felt before."

"I told you that I am in control here. There's nothing any of these sadistic wenches can do that will affect me."

The queen let out an air-slicing cackle. "Oh, yes. Stories of your womanizing are legend. I've heard about some of the amazing performances you've given. I want to see if it's true. Let me see this astounding organ of yours in action."

"The only performance you'll see is when this is over and I break your lovely neck."

"No, my friend, a man's body responds to certain activities whether his mind wants it to or not. Yesterday your mind and body worked together to withstand the torture. I will separate the two. Your body will perform exactly as I want, regardless of what your brain thinks about it."

She tapped the shoulder of female number two, and she joined number one atop the slab. Together, they launched an all-out assault upon the man's tits both left and right, licking with tongues, sucking with mouths, scraping with nails, lightly pinching and twisting between fingers and thumbs.

"Oh, my god… no… not that." Davidius lifted his head to confirm what he felt. "Why, my queen? Why are you doing this to me?"

"Why?" she returned to her pedestal and sat. "Because, Davidius, every inch of you begs to be tormented. Especially those precious knobs of yours... so stretched... so vulnerable. After all, what could be more humiliating for a man than this? Such stimulation is meant for female nipples, not male. If you want them to stop, you must answer my question. I'm sure you know what it is."

"No, damn you... never."

"Good. I will enjoy watching you writhe. Go ahead and suffer."

Davidius dropped his head with a frustrated groan, and just as he'd done the day before when enduring his torture of pain, he closed his eyes, focusing all thoughts upon withstanding this torture of degradation.

The edge of the slab cut his shoulder blades directly below his tits, which caused the orbs to be stretched and expanded to their greatest degree. Still, compared to most of the male variety his were tiny. As the female pair pinched and licked on them they became firm, their diameter shrunk and their tips rose majestically higher. Ruthlessly, the dual attackers seized upon this, grasping his raised and sensitive skin between their lips and sucking away as though expecting milk.

Never before had Davidius experienced such a feeling. It never occurred to him that his nipples could be so sensitive and respond this way. Certainly no woman had ever shown him this. When Davidius coupled with females, he was the dominant partner. He dealt the stimulation to her. He did what he pleased with her, mesmerizing her with his masculine pokes until he was finished with her. But not now. A chained man cannot dominate. He can only lay there and take whatever his female tormentors wish to give him, and what these females and their treacherous, man-tit-sucking mouths gave him was an overdose of testosterone. It raged throughout his bloodstream. Davidius felt like he was the manliest man in the world.

He opened his eyes, raised his head and watched them work him over. He unconsciously sucked in his belly and expanded his chest even higher. He strained his arms against the chains binding him, flexing himself, displaying himself, thrusting his chest towards them and offering his manly tits for them to torture. He groaned and grunted, deep-throated, like a gorilla, like a caveman, and beyond two worshiping female heads he glanced to his own head, the head of his cock in bondage. It's mushroom shape glowed a dark red, glistening and sugar coated with pre-seminal lubrication. His cock wanted to fuck. Beads of syrup emerged from its slit one after another in preparation for stimulation that was not there. He could not have what he wanted, not until she said so, and with this startling realization Davidius groaned not as a male animal but as a man frustrated. He abandoned his flexing and posing and lowered his head to inversion.

She grinned an evil grin. "Well, Davidius, does your penis still do what you tell it to do?" She motioned with finger towards a pair of women stationed near the other end of slab. They moved in and began licking the prisoner's feet, fully exposed, slightly elevated and available beyond the rings securing his ankles.

They grabbed his toes and bent them back, one on his left foot, the other on his right. They worked their tongues up and down his stretched soles, and then, using their fingers to separate his toes, they drove their tongues in between and all around each toe. Davidius did not fight them, did not try to curl his toes forward in defense. What would be the use? His feet weren't going anywhere, and besides, his initial revulsion quickly transformed into pleasure, and he arched back his toes, surrendered his feet to their mesmerizing praise.

Queen Miscreantia signaled with hand her final two tormentors. One positioned herself between the legs of Davidius and deftly maneuvered her face between two of the three chains securing his cock. She licked his testicles, his bull-sized nuts, their two-inch diameters separated by one thick line of reptilian skin. She finger-pulled his nut skin away from him and placed it in her teeth, clamping down ever so lightly. Between her fingers and thumbs she delicately tugged the hairs of his balls and scrotum, while licking, nibbling and munching with lips, teeth and tongue. Her victim did not struggle, did not flinch. He basked in her praise with eyes closed, back arched over the edge of his torture table slab of wood.

Standing on the floor beside him, the sixth female drove her face into Davidius's stretched belly. Her tongue worked into his navel and all around it, up and down, side to side, covering every inch of his well-defined muscle between sternum and pelvic bone. With her lips she grabbed his fur trail, gently tugging his hairs before saturating them with her spit. Her face plowed into his solid wall, impaling him with her nose, testing his strength by inhaling the masculine hardness of manly abdominals.

Davidius abandoned all thoughts of repulsing them. What man could fight such an erotic assault? No strength of mind could convince his body that this was unnatural and vile and should therefore be resisted. Davidius was a masculine masterpiece, virile and dominating, and so he used his manhood to fight them. He strained against his bondage. He flexed his muscles and posed for them. He arched his back and raised himself from the slab just to show them he could. He groaned and grunted and growled in voices only a man could make. He clinched his scrotum and waved his cock at them, its endless beads of pre-come flying in all directions to dot their feminine hair.

One powerful man, stripped naked, stretched wide open, bound and helpless, his mighty cock subdued in chains, did battle against six ravenous females, their tongues, lips, hands and fingers unleashed to mercilessly attack. Who would emerge the victor?

Beyond Davidius where the guards played, Lyzelma had gone silent. She no longer reacted to the repeated ravaging of her skin, nor the fucking of her pussy hole and asshole. They had used her up, but they were far from finished. Lyzelma's battle was lost, and Davidius closed his eyes, put her out of his mind lest her image weaken his resolve.

The queen rose from her chair and took a tour around the slab. She licked her lips at the sight of her prisoner's powerful yet defenseless body. She watched with delight as her experts engulfed him with their tongues, fingers and lips. And the centerpiece of it all, that beautiful, intimidating, mesmerizing man cock stood perfectly vertical, helplessly waiting for something to happen.

Her tour ended in front of his inverted face. "Davidius, we are going to play a game I call comparison and contrast. I suppose you've noticed that I am now in control of your penis. I will make it give the performance of a lifetime."

"Get on with it then, you demented fuck."

"Bring in the servant girl."

Davidius was stunned to see his good friend Celeas. Stripped naked, she descended the stairs escorted by two male guards. As the six females continued working Davidius, Celeas was allowed to kneel and speak to him. "Davidius, please forgive me. You know I have no choice in this."

"It's all right, Celeas. Don't fret. We all must suffer because of this tyrant."

The queen smiled. "That was touching. Now my dear girl, I want you to mount him."

Miscreantia summoned naked guards away from the cross and they manhandled Celeas towards the slab, while the nut-licking and belly-kissing females abandoned their positions, moving in unison to work on the calves of his legs instead. With slender scissors, the queen slid one blade between pulsating penis and restricting leather, brought the blades together and severed the cock ring.

The manhood of Davidius was set free. His mass of meat slammed onto his belly, its first contact with anything other than air for nearly two hours, which triggered a scrotum clinch that raised his cock inches above his belly to stand attentively in midair, wanting and waiting.

Guards lifted Celeas onto the slab and she wasted no time. Her feet straddled his hips. She squatted, lifted his cock with her fingers and inserted him to her vagina. He shuddered. Finally, stimulation for his tortured cock. He raised his head, observed her beyond the two still working on his tits, collapsed his head and prepared for his ride.

And ride him she did. Davidius moaned with gratified pleasure as Celeas slowly maneuvered herself up and down to inhale the power of her magnificent steed.

Secretly had Celeas longed for this. From afar she'd kept hidden her wanting of him ever since her pussy knew its purpose. She knew that one day he would tire of chasing the endless parade of meaningless women and that she, Celeas, would be unblemished and ready for him. Obviously, this was not the setting she had envisioned, but now that the moment had arrived she endeavored to make him never forget it. With the expertise of a professional, Celeas tightened her innards, nursed his massive cock, wrapped it in the warm wetness of her tight, velvety vise, crushed his thickness while increasing the pace of her up and down strokes.

Watching from a side view, the queen marveled at the straining muscles of her powerful prisoner. He flexed for her, undulated for her, tried to thrust for her in unison with his partner, but this she would not allow. "Davidius," the queen spoke with, for once, kindness. "Let her do the work. You lay back and enjoy what you feel."

Queen Miscreantia massaged her own vagina, her lubricating juices staining the center of her ivory-colored robe. She paced the floor, admiring from every angle the intensely erotic scene she'd created, and as her experts continued their relentless body worship and Celeas increased the tempo of her rhythmic fuck, the queen absorbed sights and sounds of a man tortured with pleasure and pain. Davidius emitted manly groans, writhed and flexed as he was taken to heights of ecstasy never before known to him. Davidius was close. The queen could tell, and with a shriek to crumble the stone walls surrounding them, she shouted, "STOP!"

All body-worshipers abandoned their hero, while guards violently removed Celeas from the long pole upon which she was skewered.

"NO!" Davidius howled. "What are you doing? You can't stop now, damn you."

"I said the game was compare and contrast. How can you compare until you have something to contrast it with? Was she good? You seemed to be enjoying yourself."

"Let her finish. You've got to let me get off."

"Wrong!" She stripped away her robe, climbed onto the slab and knelt onto his belly. "You will finish when I say." She squeezed his cock between her thighs. "We will work on you all day. You will tell me about Glauken or you won't. Either way, I fully intend to enjoy myself at your expense."

"You maniac," Davidius strained his arms, raised his head to glare at her. "I'm not your goddamned plaything. Let me finish now!"

"No, my friend. It is much too soon."

He collapsed with a pitiful moan. The rules were written very clearly for him. He could remain silent, or he could shoot. His cock no longer belonged to him, and in case he did not yet fully understand this, Queen Miscreantia rammed its entire eight-inch length and two-inch thickness straight up into her gut, while ordering her females to renew their attack.

And so began for Davidius his descent to hell - a torture like no other.

Every inch of his body fell prey to female hands, fingers, tongues, teeth and lips. Their assault expanded to encompass his arms, arm pits, hands and fingers. One man, stripped naked, chained and defenseless, withstood the torment of seven - no, make that eight females, as Celeas knelt on the floor before his anguished face. She unknowingly made things worse for him, kissing his forehead, nose and lips, pleading with him to surrender.

"Please, Davidius, tell her what she wants to know." She peppered him with kisses.

"Yes, Davidius," mocked the queen. "Tell me and you can shoot." She bounced on his cock, crushed him inside her. She planted both fists into his belly, using him for leverage, and just as she felt reverberations bolting the length of his shaft, she again shouted, "STOP!" and all females abandoned the slab.

"No, please no," he begged. "You can't stop now. Please, for god's sake finish me."

The queen did not answer him. Instead she joined Celeas in kneeling before his inverted face. "Well, Davidius, now your penis has felt two versions of heaven. Which one do you prefer?"

"I don't care. Just get me off."

"No, you have to choose. You must have a preference."

"Yours, my queen. Yours felt better. Yours felt like nothing I've felt before. I want you to finish me."

He lied. He didn't care. He couldn't tell the difference because this torture of denial was driving him to an ecstatic madness.

"Then I will finish you Davidius," she promised with sugary sweetness. "But first you must tell me where Glauken is hiding."

"No! I can't. Please… please don't make me."

"I'm sorry, my poor, tortured hero. You must tell me. Perhaps if I give you a third choice you can make some sort of decision."

"Oh, god no… don't do this to me."

His pleading was ignored. All mouths returned to attack, while the queen knelt between his thighs. She leaned forward, grabbed his cock head between her lips and raised it to vertical. With an opening of her jaw she swallowed him.

He twitched as though in shock, as she crushed his bulging mushroom into the back of her throat. With her tongue she scraped his shaft, manipulated his cock head with frantic slurping and sucking, and all done hands-free.

"Oh, my god, Davidius." Celeas again tormented him to surrender while smothering his face. "How long have you suffered? I cannot bear any more of it. Please, tell her. If you don't I…"

"Be quiet, damn you," Davidius interrupted with a whisper. "If you say it all will be lost. She will kill the both of us… and Glauken. Don't you know this? Now, shut the hell…"

Davidius could not finish his sentence. His nuts were under attack. Somehow, some way, the woman sucking his dick had extended her tongue to encompass his nuts at the same time. No longer was Davidius in the torture chamber. He journeyed to a far away land, a utopia of ecstasy, a realm of pleasure indescribable. He moaned an otherworldly moan. He flexed every muscle to capacity. His fingers and toes twitched. His chest rose and back arched to a torturous degree. His mighty testicles contracted to the size of harmless pebbles and his semen boiled inside their cauldron, ready to explode.

"STOP!" shouted the queen after spitting out his cock. Vile, heartless, sadistic and cruel, she again denied Davidius his end.

"God damn you to hell! You evil whore. Finish me, NOW!"

"Talk and you can shoot. It's that simple."

She did not order the other six away from him, preferring they keep him on the brink of explosion, sensing that he was near his breaking point. As she removed herself from the slab and knelt before his face, however, Queen Miscreantia learned that she was gravely mistaken.

"You must understand something, your majesty." He greeted her with a snarling show of teeth. "I will never give in to you... not to you or any woman. I'm afraid you don't know what you're dealing with. You can torture me all day... and the next day and the next, if that is your desire. I am a man. I will not be broken. I will not whimper and cower like an inferior bitch. I will stay right here and fuck you and those six and any other wench you care to throw at me. I might be chained and at your mercy; I might be unable to stop you from torturing me, but I am telling you right here and now that you will never defeat me. So go ahead and try. I will die before telling you anything."

Quite a speech, she thought, and she stood to confirm what she knew. What a man, she thought. What a fucking man he was, stretched out with his mighty chest sticking way up in the air, his tits taking a licking, his belly, legs and feet taking more lickings, his incredible phallus fully erect and ready for another round. He was right. This prisoner, this chained muscle-man, this fucking he-man was too much for any woman. Queen Miscreantia was no different than any other woman. She melted at the sight of him. Tributaries of pussy juice ran from her thighs to her toes with confirmation of it. Deny him? Impossible.

Instead, she fucked the come out of him. She rode his cock while seven females ravaged his masculine beauty. She crushed his thickness down to nothing and milked him. It didn't take long for him to shoot his long-denied load into her gut. But was she satisfied? Hell, no. Before he could even think of a come-down she released his cock from her pussy hole and recovered his cock with her drooling mouth, taking his bull nuts inside for good measure.

Torture of denial transformed into torture by milking. Davidius fired another load down her gullet, only to once again feel her velvety pussy hole crushing him with heavenly female friction. Davidius said nothing but felt everything. His mind was some place far away, some place he never wanted to leave, but as his third foaming of creamy come exploded into the queen's belly, a commotion on the stairs interrupted his ecstasy. Glauken and his men had entered the dungeon.

The queen's guards were still busy with poor Lyzelma, stark naked and with their weapons nowhere near them. They immediately surrendered.

All females had run from the slab except for Celeas, still kneeling before Davidius, and the queen, still squeezing Davidius inside her pussy hole while collapsed onto his heaving chest. Glauken approached the queen and raised his sword to strike her dead.

"No, Glauken no!" Davidius shouted. "Spare her."

"You are right, my friend. I will leave that to you. It is your right for suffering through her tortures." And with that, Glauken and Celeas proceeded to release Davidius from his chains.

"Glauken, clear this room." As he sat up, wrapping his arms around the queen to protect her, Davidius nodded his head towards the cross. "Have your men release that woman and tend to her wounds."

Glauken's men did as ordered and put the queen's people into the holding cells upstairs. Now the dungeon held only four and Davidius spoke, "Where is the queen's army?"

"We destroyed them. The few remaining have scattered to the countryside. What has this tyrant done to you?"

"Never mind that. I have a proposal. We will tell the people of our success and that the queen was killed when you stormed the casle. But I want her kept alive. We will rule as three and this woman will be kept here with us in secret. Let her keep six females of her choosing as her entourage." Davidius knew which six would be chosen.

"But why? After all she's done to our people, you want her to rule with us? Our goal was to destroy this woman and all she stood for."

"She will only be kept here for our pleasure - to make sure she never takes power again. The myth of her death will be enough to give us total rule so we can restore peace and prosperity to our people."

Glauken was still puzzled. "You say we will rule as three, but what power will this woman have?"

"Not her." Davidius turned to Celeas. "If she agrees, I will take Celeas as my wife and we three will rule this land as a triumvirate."

Celeas embraced her soon to be husband. "I will marry you, Davidius. I've loved you longer than I can remember."

"Then it is settled. There are a few people in Gaul that need to be dealt with. I will remedy that situation myself, and then we will work together to reverse the injustices done to our people here."

"I am with you, my friend. We have long waited for this day."

"Come Glauken. Let's tell the people the good news. I'll explain the rest to you later." Davidius hoped that someday Glauken could know what had been experienced in the dungeon that day.

Celeas knew. She was more than willing to accept that Davidius could never be serviced by anyone the way the former queen and her helpers had done. She would learn new techniques from this woman, learn proper uses of both her mouth and her vagina. Between them and with them, her beloved Davidius would have the best of all worlds for the rest of his days.

Fem Fist Books

Sodium Pentothal Sadists
Part 1 - What's so Funny?

I should have known the potential for disaster was there. Why wouldn't my long-time family doctor have told me that he wouldn't be in his office the day of my appointment? Certainly our relationship was such that he could have rescheduled with no argument from me. After all, it was just my annual physical, nothing I hadn't been through before. Strange, too, that the regular receptionist was not at her desk, having supposedly left early for her own dental appointment. This was told to me by a woman named Linda Carlson, who was the nurse assigned to one Dr. Helen Bracket, the substitute physician that Dr. Paige arranged to handle his afternoon appointments. Apparently, I was the last, because there were no other patients in the waiting area.

My apprehension was usurped by my desire to get this drudgery over with, so I followed nurse Carlson back to one of the examination rooms.

"Mr. Kelso," she cheerfully instructed. "Please undress and put on this gown. I'll be back in a few minutes to draw your blood."

Done and done. With my clothes neatly hung on hooks and folded in chair, I stood and waited for Nurse Linda, who told me to address her as such and sit in another chair beside the blood-draw station. She took my blood pressure reading and stuck a thermometer in my mouth. After extracting four tubes worth of blood from my right arm, she prepared my left arm for the influenza vaccination.

"But Nurse Carl... Nurse Linda, normally, Dr. Paige gives me my vaccinations. Where is Dr. Bracket?"

"Never you mind, sweetie. Dr. Bracket and I have a more efficient routine." Her smile was so charming and so soothing, I immediately felt at ease in her presence. She continued to calm me. "You can call her Dr. Helen. She has full confidence in me to get you through the routine procedures. I will have the trivial aspects of your visit completed, then she will be able to give you her intense regiment of inspections with no need to perform such trifles."

Logical, professional, and handsomely feminine in her bright, white nursing attire, Linda Carlson was a breath of fresh air, bringing a newfound enjoyment to what I had been dreading - another taxing, uncomfortable and boring physical examination. How did she do it? How did she fill me with such bliss? Such a seemingly natural and care-free attitude?

My next memory is that I was floating on a cloud and everything was, well, comical. I thought it amusing that I was laying flat, face-up on a cold, metal table. I nearly broke into laughter when I saw Nurse Linda standing above me, looking down from the end of the table while holding my hands past my head. Her little nurse's cap reminded me of a Mickey Mouse Club cap, except that it was white and had a small red cross stitched on its front. I could not contain my chuckling when I saw who I assumed to be Dr. Helen standing at the foot of the table, a sterile and cold-looking stethoscope hanging from her neck. It was nestled between her humongous boobies, the top quarters of which were exposed from a very low-cut medical smock.

I watched with glee as Dr. Helen picked up a pair of scissor and proceeded to cut away my silly gown; guffawed hysterically when Nurse Linda clamped handcuffs to my wrists and hooked the chain separating them onto a ring attached to the head of the table's base. I listened carefully for punch lines, as the doctor explained that her methods were harsh, but thorough, and that by the end of my examination she would know the precise condition of my body - its stamina; its responsiveness to various stimuli; its defensive mechanisms and ability to perform its masculine duties.

It was impossible for me to suppress my chuckling. Every statement from the doctor's lips caused my belly to jiggle. She placed her stethoscope onto one of my testicles. The initial shock of cold was soon replaced by a tickling tingle. She listened, moved the device a few inches and listened some more. She scraped it along the skin towards my other testicle, then moved it below onto my scrotum. I was giggling like a little school girl, oblivious to the tiny alligator clips being clamped between my toes by Nurse Linda.

While Dr. Helen listened to the pulse of my peter with her stethoscope, Nurse Linda hooked wires onto my alligator clips. I was informed that the veins in my penis were healthy, the flow of blood unrestricted. For this, I was thankful, so I raised my head to scrutinize its swelling. The doctor's sterile instrument was gently rubbed atop my cock head, along the top of my shaft, and when Dr. Helen removed her stethoscope, my lively penis raised up and shifted into the crook between my thigh and belly.

Nurse Linda pinned my ankles to the table with her hands and Dr. Helen examined my feet - with her nails. She scraped the soles and I broke into hysterical laughter, trying my best to draw up my legs. Nurse Linda's grip was strong. She held my ankles secure and soon my feet became accustomed to the doctor's unusual inspection.

Satisfied that my feet were strong enough to withstand her torment, Dr. Helen grabbed a reflex hammer from a drawer and returned to stand beside my groin. She lightly tapped the rubber head onto the shaft of my cock. She started just above my balls and slowly tapped her way towards my cock head. Each contact caused my dick to bounce, rising up into the air for brief seconds, then slamming down to receive another tap. This, too, gave me amusement. It also distracted me from the fact that Nurse Linda was cuffing my ankles to the table. She had split my legs and bent my knees, draping each leg on either side. With handcuffs, she clamped each ankle to metal rings near the table's base.

When the doctor quit tapping, I quit laughing, as I realized they had rendered me completely helpless. I lay atop the table from the thighs to my elbows. From there my arms were pulled down, bent backwards, with wrists cuffed. The crooks of my knees were bent over the left and right edges of the table with ankles cuffed to the sides, lower halves of my legs vertical. I was stretched rather tight, arms past my head. My rib cage was forced to rise, belly forced to flatten, and this was no laughing matter. Something told me I would not be receiving my annual flu vaccination. The effect of my drugging had vanished and when the reality of my predicament came into focus, I began to protest. This was immediately made silent by a black, leather hood placed over my head, covering it all. There were two eye holes, two nose holes and a zipper for the mouth, which was zipped shut.

A tingling between my toes accompanied the hum of a machine, and Nurse Linda stood beside the table where I could easily watch her strip down to nakedness, leaving only the cute little cap atop her head. Any resemblance to the Mickey Mouse Club was long gone.

Part 2 - Are You a Man?

They told me to be a good patient - to cooperate while they tested my manhood. Said they needed my semen and lots of it.

The doctor increased the buzz between my toes, causing them to contract upwards, arching my feet. She reached down and scraped the sole with her nails, then walked to the other side of the table and attacked my other foot in the same manner. Nurse Linda stood at the head of the table, leaned forward and dangled her tits above my eye holes. She dug her nails into my chest and belly, scraping back and forth, left and right. She mercilessly took my nipples between fingers and thumbs, pinching and twisting them like she was fine-tuning a radio. She grabbed hold of singular hairs found on my chest, on my belly, encircling my tits. She tugged on them, occasionally plucking them out of my skin.

I was taunted with verbal challenges; told that men were born to be punished; told that every man was inferior, until he could prove otherwise. I accepted their challenges, flexed my muscles. Their pain was minimized. My pleasure was maximized and I clinched my scrotum, thrusting my powerful cock into the air for all to see.

Dr. Helen transferred her scraping nails to my nuts. She ruthlessly pinched them, twisted their ever-tightening skin, plucked individual hairs from their roots, while Nurse Linda put the palms of her hands to my chest and belly, frantically rubbing back and forth, pressing down hard, setting my skin on fire.

There was elastic - or rubber. I could feel it encircling my balls, but I could not see it, because Nurse Linda's tits were pressing onto my leather mask. My face and head were drenched in sweat. My mouth yearned to break free, so my tongue and lips could taste my nurse's wonderful titties, but my garbled, verbal request was completely ignored. My testicles were bound close together, an increasing tightness distanced them from my cock. Something pulled them towards the end of the table, until my throbbing penis lifted off my belly to stand inches above it in midair. Nurse Linda removed herself from me and I raised my head to see a rubber band encircling my balls, while running from underneath was a string. It continued to the end of the table, where it disappeared, apparently tied to something below.

Then the nurse joined the doctor in a full assault. Dr. Helen stood on my right; Nurse Linda on my left. From my left, the nurse's mouth engulfed my testicles; from my right, the doctor's mouth clamped the base of my cock. I felt their tongues. I felt their lips, their warm saliva. They worshiped my manly organs, heaping their praise onto my sensitively stretched skin.

Pre-orgasmic fluid oozed from the slit of my penis head. A thin strand dribbled down onto my belly. This must have been the sign for which they were waiting, because both mouths were removed; both nurse and doctor filled their hands with alligator clips. The tiny teeth pinched the skin of my testicles; my scrotum. A plastic, adhesive-backed pad was stuck to the base of my cock, folded on either side until completing a circle around its thick meat. The male end of a snap rested on top and Dr. Helen brought an EKG-type wire and electrode, snapping it to the adhesive pad, while Nurse Linda connected wires to each alligator clip pinching into my balls.

I could not count the number of clips. I did not try. Sure, the sodium Pentothal had long ago left my system, but a new drug had taken its place. These two ladies had taken me to a level of intense pleasure and pain unknown to me. Now, it was testosterone that raged through my bloodstream - a heightened sense of masculinity. Little did I know that what I felt at that moment was just a sampling.

Switches were thrown and dials turned. The fire between my toes intensified, sending ripples through my feet, ankles and into my calf muscles. Another fire, a different fire, assaulted my testicles. It was a fire from within - a heated tingling, a maddening vibration of creepy-crawlies, as though a swarm of frantic insects had invaded my nut sac. Then, a reverberation racked the base of my cock. It contracted, but did not release. The mighty phallus stood fully erect, nearly three inches above my belly. There it remained - no relief, no relaxation, no recoil. My magnificent, manly cock was hideously tortured with electricity, locked in a perpetual contraction of voltage, masculine syrup oozing and dribbling, one bead after another.

My body reacted in kind. I arched my back, flattened my belly, expanded my chest. I posed for them. I begged them with words garbled beneath my sweaty mask, "Take me... finish me... let me shoot."

Their answer? Silence. They calmly strolled to the door, opened it and left me to writhe upon the table of examination. I was abandoned to pose and flex for myself.

Part 3 - How's My Condition?

I don't know how long they left me to writhe - could have been ten minutes or ten hours for all I knew or cared. Oh sure, it was uncomfortable and a bit painful, but all of that was unimportant, because my brain was stimulated with thoughts never before entertained. I raised my head, peeked through the eye holes of the leather hood and admired myself. Sounds arrogant, I know, but that's what they had done to me. The electrical pulses raging through my feet and legs, balls and cock had lifted me to a fevered intensity. I felt as though I was the manliest man ever born. My phallic weapon was so beautiful, standing erect, spitting it's pre-cum juices, preparing itself to do battle with these sadistic females. My testicles were swollen, engorged, filled with sperm and tingling with excitement. For the first time in a long time, the muscles in my chest and belly made me jealous. I wished that I myself could bury my own face into them - kiss them, lick them, taste their strength.

But none of my desires could be satisfied. No fulfillment could be reached without their help. This is what they had done to me. They had wrested my body from my control. It now belonged to them, and whereas logic told me that this was an undesirable situation, ecstasy told me that this event was to be relished. My impending orgasm, if and when it was granted to me, would be like none before it - an explosion of indescribable pleasure. I felt no fear from nor resentment towards my tormentors. Instead, I felt an uncontrolled lust to perform for them, to show them the potential of the masculine physique, and hopefully prove myself worthy of their praise.

Upon their return, both females were now totally naked and Dr. Helen held in her hand a giant test tube. She turned dials to intensify the electrical currents ravaging my feet, nuts and cock. Nurse Linda stood beside my chest and for her I arched my back, expanded my rib cage, flexed the muscles in my belly, arms and legs. I writhed for her; posed for her; invited her to ravage me.

With my electrified cock standing in midair, Dr. Helen covered its pulsating beauty with the test tube, and ravage me they did. From either side of the table, female lips, tongues hands and teeth assaulted my heaving chest and flexing belly. They sucked my nipples, drilled tongues into my navel, saturated the hairs on my body from crotch to arm pits with their warm saliva.

I moaned beneath my mask. Sweat was running rivers underneath the leather. I lifted my torso closer to them. Spit was coating my hairs and skin with a glistening sheen. I begged for a taste of their female flavors. I pleaded for my orgasm, but everything I said was void of conviction. My subconscious did not want this to end, even though my cock and nuts did.

My zipper was opened. Dr. Linda climbed onto the table and sat on my face, positioning her pussy hole within my tongue's reach. As I tasted her rich juices, she brought her vagina closer and pressed down, smothering my mouth with her pulsating meat. Beyond her, Dr. Helen continued to ruthlessly worship my chest and belly. I stretched myself as though on the rack, flattened my belly for her, while raising my chest for her. The tongue in her mouth heated my skin, smeared it with her saliva and my sweat. The juices flowing from Nurse Linda's vagina choked me with such pleasure that I did not notice the doctor leaving me. I was oblivious when she turned the dials to raise the pitch of humming machines.

Only when I felt the doctor's tongue licking my right foot did I realize what was happening. My electrically-charged toes were saturated with her spit, while my exposed arches were savagely scraped by her fingernails. Never in my wildest dreams could I have envisioned this being the final trigger. The pussy on my sweat-drenched face, alligators between my contorting toes, alligators biting my bulging, bound and stretched testicles, and electrode pad wrapped around my pulsating cock shaft all combined to prepare me for the inevitable. The electricity racking my scrotum, nuts and penis into constant clinching pushed me to the brink. But it was the doctor's loving assault on my poor, helpless foot that pushed me over the edge.

They showed me the tube filled with my glorious, life-giving semen, the product of an orgasmic explosion ten times greater than even I had predicted. Of course, the amount was healthy, as was I, and although I was impressed with my performance, somehow I also was a bit disappointed. My exhilarating carnival ride had come to an end, or so I thought.

Imagine my joy when the hood was removed from my head and Nurse Linda's magnificent breasts smothered my face. Imagine my elation when I saw Dr. Helen climb onto the table and insert my still electrified cock into her pussy hole. Imagine my satisfaction when I heard her pleasured screams of orgasm. And then dream of my ecstasy when the two women swapped positions and Nurse Linda used my dick to finish herself, while Dr. Helen covered my mouth and nose with her hot pussy, still buzzing from what I had done to her.

Yes, my manly phallus was used as a dildo - a very much alive dildo, active enough to contract and sacrifice yet another sample of masculine semen.

They kissed me goodbye before injecting my vein with a new dose of sodium Pentothal. I awoke in the chair where the first dose had been secretly given. They had dressed me, and in my shirt pocket was a business card.

I suppose I could have raised a fuss, complained to my regular doctor, perhaps even called the prosecuting attorney's office or board of the AMA, but I did none of that.

The card read, "Madame Helene and Mistress Linn... Trainers of SOB's... Worshipers of Real Men... (555) 555-6721. After allowing myself a week to recover, calling that number was the only punitive action I felt was necessary.

The Cave Man
Part 1 - Out of the Frying Pan, Into the Fire

Such was the life of Pete Radcliffe. For example, one minute he's dozing peacefully in the hole of a rock cliff, safely hidden from the lawmen on his trail; the next he's getting the daylights beaten out of him by a barrage of fists and feet - not just any fists and feet, but those of at least 20 females, all lily-white skinned, all naked as jay birds.

They'd pulled him out of his hole from the inside, not the out, and dragged him through a narrow tunnel into an open-spaced cavern. This is where they proceeded to stomp, kick and punch, while ripping off any piece of his clothing they could get their hands on. Packing a potent punch himself, Pete fought them the best he could, even managing to connect his own fists with a few jaws, but once one of those wild animals jumped on his back the end came quickly. Others rushed in to kick his legs out from underneath until he was down flat. Pete never had a chance. Too many numbers against him.

He never gave up, though. Every time they'd back away figuring he was licked, Pete kept trying to push up his chest and rise to all fours, fully intending to stand upright and take them on again. So, they'd have to deliver a few more stomps onto his back and force him down. Even though they lost patience with his never-ending defiance, these feminine crazies were more than impressed with his fighting spirit, not to mention his well-sculptured musculature, plentiful fur and everything else that makes a man what he is.

Eventually, the heartless females decided they'd just have to sit on him to keep him down, so after rolling him onto his back four vixens pinned four limbs, one straddled his chest with her knees and plopped her butt right down. Another did the same on his thighs.

One-hundred-per-cent worn out, Pete Radcliffe finally surrendered, wondering what these wild women planned to do next.

Now, let's back up a bit and talk about how pitiful Pete came to be in such a predicament.

Born on a mountain, raised in a cave
Clits and titties are what I crave
(Seth Radcliffe 1807-1864)

The words of Pete's grandpa repeated themselves over and over in his head, as he lay in that cliff hole half asleep, half awake. After three years of incarceration, any number of words could have been substituted to fit - tobacco and whiskey; chicken and dumplings; a bed and a bath - all would have satiated his appetite. As for his dick, anything warm, wet and tight would have felt fine indeed.

Pete, of course, didn't do what they said he did. Just like any convict, all you had to do was ask him and he'd tell you he was innocent, but in the post-Civil War, western part of the United States the word of a judge was final and that was the end of it. No appeals. No reprieves. Seven years hard labor, that's what the judge in Durango gave him for borrowing a few dollars from a "lady" living at the local house of ill repute.

Truth be known Pete really was framed, but by the Madame, not the prostitute. The expertise with which he plowed that fat, juicy cock of his into her oft-visited pussy made her feel like a woman again, rather than a slab of meat. She wanted him to stay well past the thirty minutes for which he'd rightly paid. She wanted him to take her with him when he left, but the Madame of the house was having none of that. Fifteen minutes overdue, Pete was dragged from the bed by two of her pistol-toting goons, taken into the alley way and beaten senseless.

The Madame wasn't about to punish her own property, instead concocting a charge against innocent Pete. He was immediately sent to the Montezuma County Work Farm, situated in the farthest reaches of the southwest corner of the brand new state of Colorado.

It wasn't really a farm. It was a rock quarry, where leg-ironed and most-times shirtless men swung a pick ax for no particular reason other than to fulfill their sentence of hard labor. As for Pete, he was a model prisoner - kept to himself and always followed the rules, but that didn't mean he wasn't looking for ways out. All the guards liked him, left him alone and rarely paid much attention to what he was doing. What he did do was to every day situate himself with that pick ax swinging near the horses, always hoping for some sort of commotion or distraction to make the guards pay even less attention to him.

Pete got that chance during an all-out brawl. The prisoners knew it was coming and probably the guards did too, as resentments still holding fast between former Confederates and Unionists heated to the boiling point. When it erupted, nearly 30 men on each side turned the rock quarry into chaos.

While some used fists and others swung axes, Pete bolted for the nearest mount. He grabbed hold the saddle horn, flung both legs atop the hind quarters, and with ax in hand rode towards the passageway to freedom. By the time any guard saw him, Pete was in that narrow canyon, laying flat as he could to that horse's back with rifle shot whizzing all around him. It was a good ten minutes before the riot was quelled enough for prison guards to turn their full attentions to Prisoner 216. Adding another ten minutes for them to gather a tracking guide and hunting party gave Pete Radcliffe a pretty good chance of staying gone for good.

He headed straight into Utah territory, into mountains of rock - hard to track, hard to see. Safely hidden in a tall canyon, he dismounted and prepared to lose the leg irons. Three years of practice gave him pinpoint accuracy, and with a dozen swings of the pick ax his chain was broken. Pete liked his odds as he began the pre-planned journey to find the nearest Mormon settlement available. He figured them to be not particularly fond of the United States government, and therefore perhaps sympathetic to one of its escaped prisoners. It would have worked, too, had the damned horse not stumbled on a decline and come up lame.

For 24 hours Pete used his own feet - no food, no water, no weapons, no protection from the sun. On the second day he could take no more. A crawlspace hole 20 feet up a cliff would provide protection from the blasting rays, a place of hiding from any trackers and a chance for him to sleep. He'd wait for darkness, regain his strength, and head out to resume the search for anything or anyone that might keep him alive.

Climbing up to the opening, Pete grabbed a couple of pebbles and tossed them in, making sure no critters were napping, then crawled into the darkness of shaded hole in rock. Just enough height to lay on his belly, just enough length to conceal his boots, Pete slithered to a comfortable position, folded his arms under his chin and quickly fell into a refreshing snooze.

There was no time to react, even though he heard voices beyond his head. In his tiny crawl-space, Pete could only slide backwards on his belly, but it was too late. Two hands clutched onto his right wrist, two more grabbed the left and he was dragged further into darkness, through a hole he was sure did not exist before.

He felt rock scraping his underside, as whoever held his wrists pulled him quickly deep into the cave on a gradual down-grade. A glimmer of light appeared ahead of him and Pete strained to look at his captors, but a thump on the head caused him to see nothing.

When consciousness returned he was in a small, open area of rock, just barely tall enough for him to stand up straight. When he did stand, he noticed someone had stolen his prison-issued boots and socks. He grabbed a lone torch that was stuck into a wall hole, then turned to illuminate the room, at which time he heard a softly cackling voice.

"Howdy, young feller." Sitting on haunches in one corner, a bearded man naked and furry welcomed Pete to the cave. "My name's Jack Hutch. What's yours?"

Pete stepped towards him, took hold of the scraggly beard and forced him to his feet. "What's going on here, mister?"

"Calm down, now, hot head," he chuckled with a yellow-toothed grin, "you got nothin' to fear from me. I ain't your problem."

"Then where am I and who brought me here?" Pete let go the man's beard.

"Why, you're in Utah territory, son. Thought you knew that."

Patience short, Pete again grabbed the beard. "You know what I mean. You better spill it, old man, or I'm gonna beat it out of you."

"Shit, you can't hurt me. I've done been through it all. Look around you. There's one hole in this room. Either it's a way out or a way to trouble, but one thing's for sure, it's the only way to go. So, you might as well git and leave me be."

"Sure, Jack, I'll go, but you're going ahead of me. Oh, by the way, my name's Pete Radcliffe and I'm a wanted man. Now, *you* git."

Into the tunnel they went, both bent down to accommodate its five-foot height. With Pete holding the torch, they shuffled about 20 paces before a circle of light shone from around a bend - not outside light, but a dull glow. When they were near the exit Pete told Jack to stand back, as he crouched on hands and knees to scan what was ahead. He was near another open space, cavernous and cathedral-like, lit by numerous torches protruding from sporadically-spaced holes in the rock walls. Pete crept forward, then felt the older man's foot press against his buttocks, "Go on, boy, there ain't nothing to be sceert of."

With the torch flying from his hand, Radcliffe landed on his chest with the upper half of his body laying inside the room. From each side, hands grabbed both arms and dragged him all the way in, at which time his relentless beating commenced until he ended up stripped naked and pinned down in that spread-eagle sprawl. All the time Pete was getting the crap beat out of him, Jack sat on his haunches near the tunnel and watched the show, never saying a word.

Three years of swinging a pick ax had produced a Pete strong and chiseled, but nearly two days of running from the law with no food or water had made him weak and puny. Resigned to his fate, and noticing that the females seemed to be taking a breather from their hard-earned victory, Pete inspected what he could see.

With the floor mostly flat, the ceiling of this cavern reached up into total darkness, while the rock walls were mostly pinkish and sand-colored. The entire area was rectangular, with the farthest distance between parallel walls at least 25 yards. Besides the one Pete had come through, there were two more holes big enough to enter or exit, depending on how you wanted to look at it.

Spaced willy-nilly about the walls were makeshift lean-to's of wooden sticks and cloth. Two wagon wheels were counted and some sort of pen had been cordoned off by a wood-rail fence, looking to be about 16 feet square, but with nothing inside it.

As for the women, Pete guessed there to be around 40 of those, half older and half about his age. He gazed up at the healthy blond sitting on his chest. Trim, fit, shaped with sinewy muscles, her expression was that of a savage, but natural features told Pete she was, or had at one time been, a refined and civilized girl. Being a man denied for far too many months, he automatically focused on her well-rounded breasts, soft skin and hard nipples.

It wasn't exactly a convenient moment to get aroused considering his state of vulnerability, but the touch of rough fingers rubbing on his nuts triggered an immediate response. As his penis filled with blood, he desperately turned to the only other man present.

"What is it, Jack? What do they want?"

"Well, Pete, there ain't no use me telling you just yet. They got a lot of funnin' planned, I can tell you that. Might as well just get used to the fact that these women are gonna do whatever the hell they want with ya. This is their welcoming room."

More hands joined in. They went to work on his feet and legs, while blondie scooted her butt to the end of his sternum so she could double hand-rub on his furry chest. Their hands were rough like a man's, but their techniques soft like a woman's. They were all over him, assaulting every part of his top side, except for his fully-hardened pecker that bobbed up and down on his stretched belly.

"Who are they?" he pleaded. "Do they talk?"

"That will do," came a graveled, but feminine voice. "That will do just fine."

As the massaging hands left him and pinning hands stayed, an elderly woman appeared from beyond the chest-sitting female. This woman's hair was gray and skin wrinkled. In contrast, her physique was nearly as fit as the young amazons in the group. A thin, animal-hide strip was worn around her neck, but nothing more.

"We can speak just fine, mister. Don't usually have a call to, though."

"Who the hell are you? What do you want from me?"

My name is Celeste Nehi and this is the temple of Jacob. It is named for my husband."

"I thought he said his name was Jack Hutch."

"Not him, my husband isn't here, but his spirit is. Every one of these youngsters came from the seed of Jacob Nehi. That's my daughter Sarah sitting on your chest. She was the last born."

Pete looked up at the buxom female, as she threatened him with a snarl. "I'm gonna beat the holy shit out of you."

Her first words to him, thought Pete, were not exactly an invitation to romance, or at least not to any sort of lovin' he'd been dreaming about for the past three years. "Jack," he shouted, while struggling against his captors, "what's wrong with 'em? What do they want?"

Still hunched near the tunnel hole, Jack's voice this time was stern. "Can't tell ya, Pete. Quit askin' me."

"Yes, indeedie," the old woman cackled, "that will do." She stepped back and twice clapped her hands. "Take him to the arena."

Part 2 - Corralled

They turned Pete onto his belly, brought his wrists together and prepared to lift him up, but with a renewed burst of energy, he jerked hands and feet free, then rolled far enough to get some separation from his captors. Springing to his feet, he ran for the nearest hole, plunging into darkness for but six paces, then entering another room. Cascading down the wall was clear water, which pooled into a sunken pit of grey, slimy muck. The smell of sulfur and salt penetrated his nostrils, as he searched for another means of escape, but with the possible exception of whatever was under that goo, the only way out was the way he'd come in.

With his first attempt of escaping a failure, Pete reluctantly allowed the women to escort him back to their welcoming room, to the arena, that penned area squared by four-sided wood-rail fence. Loose dirt comprised the floor, while the top rail of each side stood four feet high.

They lifted him over, tossed him inside the pen while the rest of them stood outside the perimeter both as guards and as spectators.

"You're just a firecracker, ain't ya?" mocked the grey-haired matriarch,

Celeste Nehi. "Ok, Pete..." she turned to shout at Jack. "What's his last name?"

Strolling towards the pen, he answered, "Pete Radcliffe."

"Ok, Pete Radcliffe, the rules of this game are simple. There ain't none. Whoever's pinned for a three count's a loser. No submissions. I'll start you with two and add another after a 100-count. Do what you gotta do."

The situation was hopeless. Each younger vixen stood at ringside, itching to get their hands on him, while the elders formed a second line behind them. Celeste Nehi stood inside one corner post, ready to officiate this massacre. Weakened by thirst and hunger, Pete asked for just a bit of mercy.

"Could I at least have some water before we start?"

With a sigh of exasperation, she consented. "Jack, get him a drink."

Returning with a porcelain mug full, Jack leaned over the rail and handed it to Pete, whispering, "Don't worry, boy. They won't hurt you too bad."

He gulped down the cool refreshment in three swallows, handing the mug to Jack. "More?"

"No," barked Celeste. "Sarah and Josie, you're first."

Like wild animals they leapt into the ring, slowly stalking their quarry into one corner. Pete knew only one thing - fisticuffs, and he possessed a potent punch, but these cagey wrestlers stayed out of range, tempting him to come towards the center. With the blond Sarah to his left and brunette Josie to his right, Pete crouched defensively in the corner.

Soon tired of the standoff, Celeste warned him. "The count's 30, mister. You better get busy or soon you'll be facing three."

In a flash, Pete stutter-stepped with a fencing motion towards Josie, threw a left jab that missed, then a right cross that connected with her left titty. As she howled behind him, Pete lunged towards Sarah, who deftly sidestepped his charge, extending a leg to trip him, coupled with a forearm across his back to send him crashing into the rail.

Stunned, he staggered back a few steps, where Sarah hooked her right arm with his, extended a leg and flipped him over her hip. Pete landed onto the dirt flat on his chest, as each women took hold a leg and raised them up to secure him in a double Boston crab. Leaning onto his buttocks with all their strength, the amazon duo nearly broke Pete's back in two.

"99 and 100," Celeste shouted to announce more bad news. "Marjorie, go get him."

Launching herself from the top rail, Marjorie came crashing down with both feet onto Pete's back, just as the other two released him from the crab. Three bare feet began to stomp on his backside, causing him to roll over, only to receive the same to his top side. Dropping to the dirt, Sarah quickly put the man into a brutal head scissors between crunching thighs, while Josie grabbed both ankles and stretched him lengthwise. More stomps followed, courtesy of Marjorie, to the chest, to the stomach and belly. Manly grunts and groans echoed throughout the cave, as Pete withstood this three-pronged assault. Sinewy thigh muscles clamped onto his neck cut circulation to his brain, nearly causing him to pass out, but Sarah relaxed just enough to keep him alert. She wanted him to feel every foot stomping his exposed torso.

Then, all holds were released. Pete lay spread eagle, motionless except for his heaving chest and belly. Sarah did the honors by flinging her body across his, as Celeste counted one... two... but Pete planted both feet flat onto the dirt and lifted with all his strength to send Sarah tumbling to one side.

"Well, lookee there. He did a kick-out," exclaimed Celeste. "I was hoping three wouldn't be enough. Don't want to spoil our fun." She pointed to the next opponent. "Mary, your turn."

A new attack commenced with a turning of the weakened man onto his belly. Josie grabbed both ankles, Mary got his wrists and they lifted him up, quartered and suspended in mid-air with chest hanging. Straddling him like a young steed, Marjorie sat on his back to further bend his spine downward, while Sarah slid underneath and went to work. Using short, upward jabs, she pounded into his hard, stretched abdominals, pulverizing every inch from the pit of his stomach to the lowest reaches of his belly. Deep-throated grunts coincided with each blow, as the torturous weight of the cruel mount riding his back curved his spine to a near breaking point while stretching his chest and abdomen nice and tight.

Sarah continued to launch short punches into his exposed gut, and then humiliated the poor man by grabbing both nipples between fingers and thumbs. Mercilessly, she gave him double titty-twisters, causing the titty owner to howl with grief. After a few more hard knocks to his middle section, Sarah rolled out from underneath, Marjorie dismounted and the other two dropped him like a rock. Pete crashed chest-first into the dirt.

They rolled him over and again Sarah draped herself across his prone body for a count of one... two... and another defiant kick-out.

"Well, god damn, Pete," Celeste complimented. "Maybe you're not such a sissy-boy after all. Bridget, see if you can finish him off."

Jack stood behind the leader, proud that this fellow was holding up to the brutal assault of four, soon to be five, young women. All these vicious females working on one helpless man, yet he continued to find enough strength to rebuff their attempted pins. As he watched Pete push upwards with his arms in a struggle to rise, Jack shouted out words of encouragement. "Don't give up, Pete. Show 'em what a man can do."

A few stomps to the back sent Pete chest down onto the dirt, then Sarah pounced on top of him. She hooked her arms underneath his, brought hers up to lock her hands behind his neck, then pulled up his arms to secure him in a full nelson. With one swift jerk, she rolled over onto her back, bringing Pete with her to lie atop and crush her bulbous titties. She pulled his arms down with ruthless authority, while pressing the back of his neck with her locked hands. Marjorie and Josie each grabbed an ankle to stretch him lengthwise, adding further agony to an already painful hold.

This poor man lay there groaning in futile agony, as his back arched, chest thrust upwards and middle section collapsed from the merciless full nelson. Two women who had nothing to do knelt on either side of Pete's expanded rib cage, not to inflict more pain, but torment. Two hands lay flat onto his rippled belly; two more frantically rubbed his heaving chest. One man versus five women, Pete never had a chance. His cock instantly sprang to life and flipped from down to up. Lips touched the pit of his stomach and furred chest, and along with it came a slight protest. "He stinks."

"That's right, Bridget," the matriarch soothed. "He smells like a man. The man we've been waiting for. Use your tongue, ladies. Lick him clean. Spit on him so he don't smell so bad."

All 20 of the younger females entered. Each surrounded the man, as many as could kneel beside him, and proceeded to lick away all dirt, all sweat, all slime.

"Not the penis," Celeste warned. "Make him wait."

One man versus a gaggle of lustful women, Pete writhed in ecstatic torment.

He felt the smashed titties and hard nipples of Sarah grinding into his back muscles, while countless tongues moistened every inch of his top side. Fingers and thumbs delicately pinched and twisted the skin of his testicles, while frothing spit darkened manly fur. They sucked on fingers and toes, slimed his arm pits, licked and lip-pinched his nipples, tongue-drilled his navel. They taunted and teased with their titties, dangling the soft balloons within inches of his mouth, but never allowing his yearning tongue to touch or taste.

As the intensity increased, so did the gyrations of his cock. Nobody touched it, but all were mesmerized by its powerful ballet. Thick, sturdy, fully engorged with veins pulsating just beneath its surface, this man's mighty tool helplessly bobbed and weaved, aching for attention. Its owner undulated, near madness as he pitifully gazed upon countless tits and pussy holes, so close, yet so out of reach.

How long had these ravenous females waited for the muscled, fur-covered skin of a strong, virile man? Countless drops of vaginal juices dotted both dirt and man, as newfound exhilaration, along with long-forgotten pleasures overwhelmed every female present.

Jack Hutch rather enjoyed this scene himself. He climbed into the ring for a closer look, calmly standing beside Celeste while cupping her once-beautiful breast into his palm. "I'd say you struck it rich," he whispered.

"He's a healthy one, Jack. That's for sure."

They both gazed upon the relentless female feast of a helpless man's flesh, focusing on their victim's neglected cock, its head now fully encased with pre-orgasmic ooze. "How long you gonna make him wait, darlin'?"

She smiled while grasping onto Jack's other hand, bringing it to cup her other breast, answering him as he moved behind her. "Guess 'til I get off myself, Jack. Then I'll think about Pete."

Jack dropped one hand, inserted three digits and finger-fucked her glistening vagina. Low-pitched moans rumbled from her chest, as Jack expertly found her vibrating clit and rubbed her there. Increasing the pace, Jack rapidly massaged back and forth, causing shudders to reverberate throughout her body.

"You're a brute, Jack Hutch. Oh, god, just think of what might have been."

His finger attacked like a jack-hammer, ruthlessly vibrating her spongy clit from front to back and side to side. "It's gonna work out just fine,

Celeste… better than you could've hoped… maybe."

Her body tensed for orgasm, but Jack's hand never let up, not even after a second volley quickly followed the first. "Jesus Christ, Jack, hold me before I collapse."

He propped her up with the cupped-under-breast hand, while slowing the pace with his rammed-up-the-pussy fingers. "Want me to hand-job him?"

"No, better let me. The girls wouldn't understand."

"He won't understand it either way."

With Jack's hands removed from her, Celeste stepped towards the ravenous females. Like vultures they fought one another for access to their defenseless prey. They had brought him to an uncontrolled state of madness, to the point that Sarah's full-nelson was no longer necessary, not that she released it.

He arched his back to a torturous degree, thrusting his powerful chest high into the air. He physically invited the tongues to lick. He writhed in unbridled lust, begging their lips, hands, tongues and fingers to mercilessly squeeze, kiss, slurp and rub. With each exhale, he flattened his belly and held it there as long as possible. He tempted them to bury their faces deep into its hard muscle. He yearned for tongue tips to pile-drive their way deep into his knotted navel.

For Jack, the view was beyond belief. One incredible man - stripped naked, held in a torture rack grasp, hopelessly outnumbered, assaulted by crazed, starving, mouth-drooling, pussy-dribbling females. Poor Pete undulated heroically, sacrificing his manly form to their torments. Jack could hear the slurps, nearly feel the slurps. He jealously watched full-blown breasts hovering near Pete's face, as Pete gallantly but uselessly struggled to devour each one of them.

For three long years Pete's only company was other men. Three years since

Pete had even smelled a woman, let alone felt her touch or tasted any part of her. Now, an overdose, so tantalizingly close to fulfillment, yet so cruelly denied him. Despite this teasing torment, Pete never said a word, never begged for his release or complained about his predicament. Although these females outnumbered him, punished him, controlled him, they never defeated him. Pete Radcliffe remained a man, groaning and grunting and writhing and taking everything they so far had dished out.

Then, the two men locked eyes. Jack smiled. Pete moaned. "How long they gonna torture me, Jack?"

"Wrestling's fun, ain't it boy?"

Before he could answer, titties were replaced by a juice-drenched pussy hole, as a young daughter of Jacob Nehi lowered herself onto Pete's face. He inhaled the horrendous smell - the heavenly, horrendous aroma of athletic female loins. His tongue snaked into her darkness, searching for a little peter, already engorged and awaiting his touch. And just when he found it and her body convulsed, the hand of Celeste encircled Pete's tormented cock and gingerly finger-massaged its swollen head.

For a man who stood at a height of five feet and ten inches, Pete was a lucky fellow to be endowed with a double-fister. Not only was it a fat and juicy one at three-quarters of an inch thick, Pete's cock extended a full five inches above the four fingers of Celeste, making a grand total of nine inches in length. Its hammer-head was a handsomely sculptured mushroom, its rim casting a full half-inch shadow on the shaft below, and with a woman's fist squeezing that shaft his mushroom bulged, darkening its color from pink to red as beads of pre-come oozed out of the slit to make him shine with a sugar coating.

Celeste liked it. She said, "Daughters of Nehi, behold."

A reverent hush enveloped the room and all faces were removed from the man's body. Fingers pinched his tits and hands massaged his chest, belly, legs, and feet, while a gaping pussy hole covered his mouth. Spectators hand-rubbed their own vaginas, marking time with legs as though they had to pee, as Jack stroked on his own hardened pecker. All eyes focused on Pete's cock and a woman's hand to see Pete fire an initial volley past the hands on his belly, past the hands on his chest, splattering onto the lower back of the face-sitting female. A second bullet slimed the hands on Pete's chest, while subsequent contractions produced a dotted trail of semen from the hands on his stomach to his belly.

Celeste squeezed on Pete's powerful cock from base to head, crushing out all remaining man-seed, and then she delicately laid the mighty weapon to rest.

Pete glared at the elderly woman, thrusting forward his lower jaw while flexing his chest. It was a display of defiance, a statement, and if there was any doubt remaining for her as to what sort of character had stumbled into her clutches, Pete verbalized it for all of them in a mocking tone. "You beat on me, torture me for hours, and the best you can do is a hand job? You ain't no ladies. You're all a bunch of losers."

Celeste cackled with glee. "Tie his ankles and get him ready. We've found us a real man."

Fem Fist Books

Part 3 - Everybody Wants Some Man-Meat

They lifted and carried Pete back through the hole from where he'd come, back to the little room where he'd met Jack. Here, they sat him on his butt and gave him water, of which he drank plenty. As the last female stepped toward the exit, Pete asked with the sweetest voice he could muster, "Miss, could I get something to eat? I'm powerful hungry."

She didn't even bother to turn around, instead disappearing into the tunnel as though she hadn't heard him at all. With nowhere to go and nothing of promise to look forward to, Pete fell onto his side and quickly collapsed into a deep slumber. No memories of grandpa Seth this time. Finally, Pete Radcliffe could sleep in peace, figuring this form of incarceration was a far cry better than the one he'd left behind in Colorado.

It was a long while before he was stirred from his coma. Pete had dreams - fantasies of those female hands all over him, but this time they were smooth as silk, almost like they were velvet-gloved. He felt them all over his back side from head to toes and in the butt crack. He felt them on and in between his fingers, arms and pits, chest, belly, thighs and calves. He especially felt them on his balls and cock, where they seemed to linger for an awfully long and pleasurable amount of time, before he was jolted from this soothing dream world by a drenching of water.

Pete sprang up to sit on his butt just as another bucket was poured onto his head. Two more came flying from either side of him, as the ladies rinsed away the last of his stink. Without a word, they one by one disappeared into the tunnel, leaving Pete alone, dripping clean and starving worse than before.

"Feel better?" Jack's voice came from the shadows. He stood and walked towards Pete. "C'mon, let's get you more comfortable." Lifting under the armpits, Jack maneuvered the ankle-bound man to a wall and brought his back to lean up against it. "Are ya hungry, boy?"

"Hungry ain't the word for it, Jack."

"I'll fix ya right up." He headed for the far wall, lifted the lid off a small black kettle and spooned some sort of stew into a bowl. Bringing the meal closer, Jack could barely let go before Pete yanked away the bowl to shovel every drop into his mouth. No time to chew, he swallowed it whole and licked the bowl clean, all gone in 30 seconds.

"More, please," Pete asked, noticing that the bowl was of an indoor type, made of porcelain with a fancy border. The spoon looked to be of a fine silver plating, now tarnished.

"Like it, do ya?" Jack smiled while serving up another helping.

"Right now, I'd like just about anything you wanna give me. What is it, anyway?"

"Well, Pete," he chuckled. "What critters do you know of that live in a cave?"

"Hell, I don't know." He slurped one spoonful after another, this time allowing his tongue to get a taste before sending it down the hatch. "Spiders, snakes, birds, bats... what else you got?"

"That about covers it. Could be any or all of 'em."

Pete stopped, thought about it, then continued to devour. "Where'd you get the fancy dishes?"

"God damn it boy," he whined in a good-natured way. "Don't start up again."

"Sonuva bitch, Jack, can't you tell me anything?" He spit beads of stew, clearly frustrated. "And quit calling me boy. I'm a grown man, for Christ's sake."

"Ah, hell, Pete, I'm sorry." Jack dropped his head. "I know you're a man. One hell of a man. It's just that you remind me of a young man I used to run with, that's all. Back in my prospectin' days."

"You were a prospector? For what?"

"Any metal worth anything. I was hopin' for veins of copper or silver when I crawled in to take a look at that hole."

"You mean the hole I was in?"

"Yep. They dragged me out... or in, just like they done you."

"What'd they do to you?"

"Oh, they had big plans for me, Pete. I done fucked every one of 'em time and again, but all they got was..."

"What?" he asked while handing the bowl over for a third helping. "What'd they get, Jack?"

"Ah, hell," Jack dejectedly answered. "It ain't somethin' I'm proud of." He handed Pete another dose of stew, then sat beside him. "Let's just say they got their own satisfaction. Still do, when I'm up for it, which is most the time."

"Why didn't you help me, Jack? Why'd you let them beat the hell out of me?"

"Because I went through the same thing. No one helped me. Besides, I know where this is headed. The worst is over. Don't worry, Pete. We men gotta stick together. We'll be fine."

Pete struck Jack's thigh with a good-natured slap. "Guess I'll have to trust you. Got no other choice."

"That's right," Jack chuckled, while returning the thigh slap. "You know, Pete, prospectin's a lonely business. That young feller I ran with was about your age. Name was Rodney, but I called him Rod. You know why?"

"I dunno. Nickname?" he guessed between slurps of stew.

"Partly, but more because I thought he had just about the purdiest pecker I'd ever laid eyes on. Balls, too. When Rod was hangin' with me, he was never wantin' for nothin'."

"Took good care of him, did you?"

"Had to. Nobody else around for a hundred miles. Situation like that, men gotta stick together... like I said."

Pete never flinched when Jack's hand cupped Pete's balls. He merely continued to empty his bowl.

"Yep. Watchin' you perform for the ladies brought it all back. Your dick's just as handsome, but you got purdier nuts. Big and juicy they are."

"I can't believe they hand jacked it." He sat the dry bowl to the ground.

"All those women and not a one of them took me up their twat or in their mouth. Kinda disappointing."

"Ol' Jack will take care of that," he whispered, while bringing his second hand to gently clutch the spongy cock-shaft. "If you'll let him."

Pete never said a word, instead pressing his hands to the dirt and maneuvering himself away from the wall. "Sure, Jack. Have at it."

Pete lay flat on his back, sprawling his arms past his head. With ankles bound in rope, Pete drew up his knees like a butterfly, giving room between his thighs for Jack to get at his ball sac. Just the thought of having a warm, wet tongue on his nuts and pecker had Pete 50 percent hard already, and he closed his eyes to enjoy whatever service Jack could come up with.

"God damn it, Jack," echoed the piercing voice of an old woman. "What the hell are you doing?"

"Celeste... I was just gonna ..."

"Gonna what? Drain him? You were warned, Jack Hutch."

A gaggle of females surrounded and grabbed hold, dragging Jack to the tunnel, but not before he could blurt out to Pete, "Son, don't believe what you see. I ain't as old as you think." He continued to shout as they disappeared into darkness. "I can still screw with the best of 'em. You'll see, I ain't licked yet." Jack's voice faded away, his information only further confusing Pete as to what the hell this was all about, so he asked.

"Damn you, Celeste Nehi, what the hell is this all about?"

"Pete Radcliffe, you may think you're a big man, but you ain't shown me nothing yet." The old gal seemed to be in a sour mood. "Should've known I couldn't trust that old fool. Or you neither. Men! Bah! So typical. Understand this, Mr. Pete Radcliffe. Women rule here. This is *my* temple. You and Jack will learn the hard way what happens to men who desecrate my temple."

With a snap of her fingers, stomping feet rained down on Pete, while Celeste urged him to fight back. Of course, he did the best he could for a man outnumbered and bound with ankle rope, but just as before, exhaustion did him in.

They left him prone on his back for a few minutes until his panting for air slowed a bit, then in a flash Pete was lifted up by the arms and bound ankles for transport with his butt hanging. Back through the tunnel, they brought him into the welcoming room where he heard a commotion over by the pen. Another wrestling match was taking place and it looked like Jack was in the middle of it, but the entourage was too far away for Pete to be sure. Of one thing he was certain, whoever was in the middle of that pen was getting the holy crap beaten out of him, something with which Pete was all too familiar.

"Take him to the dipping room," Celeste shouted from behind, and the group exited the main area. Directly into that tunnel they went and when they emerged, Pete saw Sarah and two others standing knee-deep in that grey, slimy pool of nose-burning muck.

"Cut his ropes and toss him in."

Pete squirmed in a desperate struggle to break free, but with two females assigned to each limb, all he could do was helplessly hang as they swung him towards the slime and let go. He splashed into the pool seat first, gravity taking him below the surface to crash land onto his butt. With palms flat, Pete sat in the thick, salty-sulfur-smelling but soothingly-warm slime, which covered every part of him but for his head and shoulders. Before he could react, Sarah put him in a headlock while the other two secured kicking legs and swinging arms. They wrestled his head under the surface and held him there for several seconds, then raised him up coughing and gasping for air.

"C'mon, you mouse," Celeste mocked. "Fight for your life."

Again they tried to dunk him, but Pete managed to lock both arms straight onto the solid rock floor to keep his head above the gunk. Twisting and pulling with the leverage of a professional, Sarah inched his mouth closer and closer, while the others pushed on his legs and torso, rolling him over to endure another dunking. And so, mud wrestling ensued. Three women against one man, as Pete was repeatedly taken down to ingest slick, salty, sulfuric muck.

He gallantly fought with everything he had. He kicked, he punched, he squirmed, but the result was always the same: another dunking for Pete. Exhausted, his resistance faded to that of a little boy as Sarah held firm around his head and they kept him under for nearly ten seconds. They raised him. He coughed and recovered. They dunked him again for another ten before letting him up from that foul-smelling and worse-tasting gunk. He coughed and spewed the nasty liquid from his mouth, nearly gagging from the burning brine and fumes that came with it.

"That'll do, girls. Put him in the nook."

They brought him to a cornered area, draped his arms outside the pool to rest on the rock surface, while supporting his buttocks with their arms underneath. Two females outside the pool grabbed Pete's wrists and lifted him out to lay spread eagle on hard rock.

"I think you've swallowed enough. Does it taste good?"

Constantly spitting out grey goo, he continued to gag and did not answer, but he sensed a throbbing cock and lifted his head to confirm it.

"I see you like wrestling with my girls," she laughed.

They rubbed that slick muck deep into the Pete's pores, which only further intensified the strength of his throbbing tool. Pete lay flat to enjoy the sensations of countless massaging hands, hoping, but not asking, that one of them would either mount, suck, or at the very least take his dick into their fist for some tantalizing masturbation. Nobody touched poor Pete's beautiful cock.

With a clap of their matriarch's hands, all females rose to their feet and stepped back from the prisoner, leaving him to lustfully writhe on the stone floor.

"I think he's fired up plenty," Celeste taunted. "Time to try him out."

Part 4 - Spinning the Wheel

Bringing buckets of water, the women drenched Pete's undulating form to rinse away grey goo, then carried him out suspended by four limbs. For the first time, Pete entered room number four, where he was reunited with Jack Hutch.

Here were the other two wagon wheels, both still attached to their axles. They'd been rigged so that the axles were set horizontally into grooved, wooden stands and counter-weighted with heavy rocks bundled by rope netting. These bundled rocks were suspended by one strand of rope from each bundle, looped over the axles at opposite ends to the wheels. This made the wheels stand vertical with their lowest edge about ten inches off the cave floor. The wooden stands holding them, along with the bundled counter-weights, allowed the wheels to spin just as if they were attached to the wagon from which they'd come.

"Howdy, Pete," Jack chuckled. "Did you eat lots of that grey shit?" His light-hearted question was asked from a seemingly dire predicament: Jack Hutch, stripped naked, was bound to one of the wheels.

His legs were spread wide and ankles extended just outside the rim, his legs secured by ropes wrapped around his shins and through spokes of the wheel. Also tied in ropes were Jack's wrists. With his hands folded behind his head and wrists bound together, another rope secured his wrists to the rim of the wheel, leaving the crown of his head to rest against the palms of his hands.

And as if this bondage wasn't precarious enough, Jack Hutch was upside down. With his buttocks covering the center hub, causing his pelvis to be thrust forward, Jack's naked body was inverted while his healthy scrotum hung handsomely vulnerable. His cock also hung exposed. And speaking of handsome, gravity brought this old man's fuck tool in a straight line down his belly clear past his belly button. That's not all. His scraggly beard was gone, shaven clean, and with this new appearance Jack Hutch looked to be mid-forties at most.

"Well, no need to answer," Jack laughed while focusing on Pete's engorged cock. "I can see you've done been dunked."

"Upright him," Celeste ordered. "Having fun, Jack?"

"You know it, mama. I aim to please."

"Ok, girls," Mrs. Nehi barked. "String that one up like this one."

Pete Radcliffe was fixed to the second wheel, bound in the same manner as Jack in an upright positon.

"Get ready for a wild ride, son." Jack smiled.

"I'm afraid to ask you, Jack, but what the hell is this all about?"

"This here cave's got four rooms that we know of, Pete. There's the waitin' room where you met me; the welcome room where you got to wrestle; the skinny dippin' room where you got dunked; and this."

"What's this? The torture room?" Pete gazed to his male companion, as the females tied the final knot of his ropes.

Jack laughed, "Well, maybe, dependin' on how you wanna look at it."

"Ok, I get it. You can't tell me."

Both men looked at one another. Two men, separated by about six feet, bodies spread wide, turned upright and vertically bound to their wheels, Jack and Pete scanned each other's naked bodies.

"No, Pete, I can't say anything. Don't wanna scare you."

Jack's impressive tool pointed straight forward, piercing nearly eight inches of air, while Pete's, surprisingly to him, also remained as hard as when he'd left the dunking room. Being with Jack comforted Pete. He figured that regardless of whatever tortures lay ahead for him, at least Jack had been through and survived them. More importantly, Pete felt a bond with this man. For whatever reason, Jack's presence allayed his fears. He'd guided Pete through one mysterious ordeal after another and Pete reckoned that as long as they were together they could handle whatever punishments these vixens cared to throw at them.

He tested the ropes and their knots, flexing and straining to see if they'd give. Of course, they didn't, but his efforts certainly excited his spectators. Pete's masculine form, still defiant, bound and helpless with manly tool primed for action caused a stir amongst the ladies. His body still glistened with a combination of water and sweat, his dark brown hair sparkling with tiny beads from the top of his head to the tops of his feet. With Pete performing as the lust-crazed, masculine beast he was, 80 female hands self-massaged 40 female pussies. With Jack joining Pete to display his own strength, clenching his scrotum to make his cock bob up and down and wave to the ladies, 40 fingers fingered 40 clits and 40 streams of vaginal juices began to trickle.

After two wooden stools were placed on the floor in front of Pete, Celeste tapped the shoulder of the youngster, Josie. This pretty brunette stepped up with one foot on each, then took Pete's throbbing cock into her hand, holding it steady while she covered him with her pussy hole. Finally, Pete felt the loving warmth of a vibrating vagina. She clinched her interior muscles to squeeze his pulsating pole, then threw back her arms, locking her hands behind her head.

Sarah, the muscular blond, spun the wheel. Pete spun with it. Two voices, one male and one female, let out slight whimpers, as a tantalizing sensation stirred their innards. Sarah increased the speed of revolution. One turn outpaced the next, as animalistic howls echoed from one rock wall to another. Pete's body became a blur, while Josie arched her back and thrust forward her pelvis, driving Pete's frantically rotating cock into her pussy for maximum penetration.

For Pete, the penis wasn't the only thing spinning. His head became lighter than air and all vision became white. All he could feel was the indescribable ecstasy of this rotating fuck. Spinning friction of warm wetness consumed and lifted him to a frenzied state of unbridled masculinity.

Two voices cried out words of English, "Oh, god; holy shit," coupled with sounds and utterances known only to sexual climax, as man and woman spewed their orgasmic fluids, dual eruptions and emotions never before felt.

Sarah let go the handle. Revolutions slowed. Pete's body stopped with his feet up and head down. Ecstatic moans filled the room, as Josie withdrew her pussy, uncovered Pete's cock and stepped down from the stools. Reaching for the rim, Josie turned the wheel to bring Pete upright, where he gasped for air, hypnotized with lust.

"There ya are, Pete," Jack's voice of joy brought everybody back to reality. "This here's the milking room, but there ain't no cow teats to milk - just man dicks."

"That's right, young man," Celeste joined in. "And that's exactly what we're going to do. Marjorie, you're next."

Still primed and ready, Pete's poker again was covered by another salivating pussy hole and the wheel turned to produce the next psychotic, wall-crumbling, double-orgasmic explosion of animal sounds and human creams.

They left him upright, chest heaving, with manly tool still primed for action.

"Lookin' good, Pete," Jack chuckled. "I think you'll be makin' up for those three years of nothing to fuck, you fornicatin' he-man."

Contrary to what should have been, Pete felt like a sex-crazed, nut-busting maniac. He expanded his chest, sucked in his belly and thrust forward his cock while grunting like a caveman, "Ugh… bring it on, woman."

Celeste prompted Bridget to take a ride on the spinning cock, but as she mounted Pete and Sarah turned the handle, Josie dropped to her knees in tears.

"Momma, I did a bad thing."

Celeste comforted her daughter, lifting Josie to stand while her other daughter shrieked with delights of spinning Pete-meat. "What is it, my darling?"

"I put my fingers in that hole." She pointed to Sarah. "I put my tongue in there, too."

"Yes, Josie, that is bad, but only because you and Sarah did not ask me first. You have confessed. You are forgiven."

As Josie walked away, Marjorie took her place to confess all of her sins, following it up with a pleading. "Momma, you've got to let Pete go. He's the most amazing man we could ever hope for. Please stop torturing him."

"All right, dear. You're a good girl. We're not torturing Pete. Look at him. He's a happy man."

Indeed he was. With a third orgasm completed and cock aching for another round, Pete writhed in a frenetic ecstasy. He looked to his buddy. "Shit, Jack. Ain't you gonna get some?"

"I don't know, Pete. What about it, Celeste? Send one of them old birds up here. I'm ready to go."

"You old lecher," she bellowed. "You're always ready to go."

She directed an old one to step up for a ride on Jack's pole, but had a surprise for Pete. "Bring in our prisoner."

Into the room came another naked man, groggily stumbling between the grasping hands of two daughters. "Hey, I know that fellow," exclaimed Pete. "That's Bart Conroy, from Montezuma County."

"Yes, Pete," Celeste confirmed. "We dragged him out of that hole same as we did you. Been wrestling him ever since. He claims he's the tracker from that prison you were in."

"Right as rain, that's exactly who he is. How long has he been here?"

"Jack heard a rustling when we were giving you a bath and you were asleep."

She gazed over to Jack, who was wildly spinning on the wheel, whooping and hollering on his orgasmic merry-go-round. "Jack went up there and dragged that tracker in all by himself. Jack's one hell of a man, but he's got no sperm. He can fuck like a mad dog, but nothing comes out."

Grunts, screams and moans confirmed it, as Jack's spinning cock contracted blanks and his aged girlfriend spasmed real juice.

"Are you satisfied, Maggie?" Jack chuckled as the wheel came to a halt.

The poor thing nearly collapsed, forcing the others to rescue her in their arms. She babbled ecstatically, "Oh, my god. What a fucking man. Lordy, lordy, lordy, I love that man's cock."

As for Jack, he posed just like Pete, puffing up his broad chest, sucking in his thick and well-sculpted belly, begging for more. "Gimme anothern, Celeste. I'll fix all of 'em good."

Pete broke into laughter, "Me, too, Celeste. Gimme anothern."

Jack got his wish, but Pete got something else. "Got to try something first, young man. This Conroy fellow's got some learning to do. Back him up there, ladies."

They pounced on the weakened man like carnivorous beasts, lifting him up with his knees bent and thighs spread wide. Conroy was tilted so that his upper torso was horizontal while the rest of him was vertical position, chest down, waist bent, and arms pulled past his head by hands holding his wrists. He was shaped like an L turned to the right. One of the females spit on her hand and rubbed her slickum onto Bart's anus, while another did the same with her spit onto Pete's hard pecker. Then, they impaled Bart Conroy onto Pete's dick.

Pete could not have cared less. For him, in his state of lustful craziness any hole would do, but for the owner of that hole it was a different matter. Conroy howled in ungodly pain, as female youngsters mercilessly thrust his ass onto the pole, sending Pete's ram-rodding tool past the man's rim with no regard as to Bart Conroy's comfort. There was no time for him to do anything but scream, as that fat and impaling cock was buried to the very depths of Conroy's bowels.

"Ok, Sarah, give Pete a whirl. Ladies, hold that ass steady."

Pete loved it. Mr. Conroy's virgin ass was just as tight as any pussy he'd ever felt and the increasing revolutions gave him all the friction he needed. Another orgasmic rocket flooded Bart's rectum, as he let out howls worthy of a bitch in heat.

When the wheel stopped, they yanked his ass free of Pete's cock just as violently as they'd connected it, and then laid Conroy on the floor chest up with arms and legs pinned.

"Make sure that asshole stays closed," Celeste chuckled. Fists planted firmly to the sides of each butt cheek did the trick, as they kept Conroy's ass shut tight.

Bridget stood before her mother. "I did a bad thing..."

"I know," Celeste interrupted. "We all have done bad things. I forgive you."

The elderly ladies weren't paying much attention to all of this, because they were busy taking turns on Jack's carnival ride, and as for Pete, he was feeling no pain. "Ok, Celeste. Who's next? Man? Woman? I don't care."

"I know you don't, Pete. Do you know why?"

"Can't explain it." He expanded his chest and thrust it towards her. "Wanna lick me? I feel like the horniest fella who's ever born."

She burst into laughter. "You *are*, Pete. You *are* the horniest, and the manliest man ever born, because of that gunk you swallowed. As long as that grey mud is in your belly, nothing's going to stop you from shooting one load after another. Let me show you something else, too."

Celeste stepped onto the stools, then reached up with both hands to take Pete's manly nipples between fingers and thumbs. With a violent pinch, she twisted both, clamping with all her strength. "This ought to hurt. Does it?"

"No, I don't feel much of anything there."

"How about this?" She reared back and punched him in the belly as hard as she could. Fist met muscle with a deep thud, but all Pete could do was laugh.

"Stop it, woman. That tickles."

"That goo protects you from pain... deadens it. All you feel is your masculine sex drive. Now, feel this."

She returned to his tits, but this time her fingers lovingly squeezed and rubbed on them.

"Holy shit! My dick just got bigger."

"No, it can't get any bigger," she chuckled, while moving forward to mount him. "It just feels that way. Like a man. That's all you can feel."

"You don't need to spin me, Celeste. Just do that nipple thing. I'll do the rest."

"Oh, we can do better than that." She felt the amazing strength of the man all pinpointed to one place: his powerful cock, fully imbedded to her crushing vagina. "Daughters of Nehi, join us. Set Jack free. The man we need is right here."

Celeste stood clamping Pete in her magical vise while tenderly stimulating his ever-shrinking tits. Within seconds, molestation commenced. Pete arched his back, sucked in his belly and thrust forward his chest, as a plethora of tongues, lips, hands and fingers enveloped him. With the exception of those females securing Conroy, they all had a taste of Pete wherever they could find an available piece of Pete's skin. All females took their turns. All females ravaged him. All females lavished Pete Radcliffe with the praise only a man such as he deserves. And all the while, the vagina of Celeste squeezed and comforted his mighty cock inside her warm, velvety vise.

From behind, Jack positioned the stools from his wheel so he could step up to work on Celeste. He massaged the breasts of the matriarch, delicately rubbing and pinching her hardened nipple tips. Pete's incredible tool surged to spread her vaginal walls, and she clamped her inside muscles as tight as she could to steady herself.

"I'm ready," she moaned. "Leave him be." All tongues were removed. "Send him."

The wheel was given a sudden spin. Pete's powerful pole whirled inside her, and the poor woman shuddered. "God, Jack, hold me tight. We done found us a he-man. There's nothing in the world like this. Pete Radcliffe's got the cock to beat all cocks. He's the most... incredible... oh, my god... what a fucking... man... what a... fuck... ing... god... damn... ma... ah... uh..."

Only Jack's hands clamped to her breasts kept Celeste upright. Every muscle, every nerve in her body twitched and convulsed, as Pete's magical seed jettisoned deep into her bosom - his cock's fat, powerful thickness violently corkscrewed her vibrating pussy hole. Lustful, indescribable sounds connected to some pre-historic civilization nearly crumbled the rock walls surrounding them. Pete Radcliffe and Celeste Nehi had returned to a time when Neanderthals ruled the earth. The Caveman, dominant and indestructible, wholly conquered his female tribe.

The wheel did eventually stop and Jack tenderly removed her from Pete's forever-throbbing manhood. He gently laid Celeste on the floor and cradled her in his arms. "We done good, darlin'," Jack comforted her. "Jacob's smiling down on us right now."

"And it works," Celeste gazed up at him. "Doesn't it, Jack?"

"We're about to find out just how good."

Part 5 - Pete Radcliffe: He-man of the West

"Well, Celeste," Jack stroked her silvery hair through his fingers. "We got one problem left to fix. Let's see if our grey goop can help us out."

Jack coaxed his woman to stand with him above the still-pinned-to-the-floor Bart Conroy, but before either of them could ask him anything, Conroy blurted out a secret.

"I kilt a man back in Salina, Kansas."

"Oh, did ya now?" Jack chuckled. "Did they catch you?"

"No. Was an accident. We was ridin' out to…"

"We don't need the story. You killed him and never told nobody. Ain't that right?"

"Yep."

"What do ya think we oughtta do about it? There's about 40 witnesses just heard you say that."

"I dunno. What do ya wanna do?"

Jack looked to Celeste. "Works like a charm. Guess we're all set."

"Yes, we are. Tell him, Jack."

"Well, Bart, we could turn you in… that is, unless you'd like to do us a little favor."

"I suspect I will. What is it?"

"Pete Radcliffe is dead. You saw his body at the bottom of a ravine, or at least what was left of it after the wolves and turkey vultures had their fill. Fell he did. Tumbled about a hunnerd feet. Ain't that right?"

"Come to think of it, I did see a man's body. All that was left was bones and prison garb. That must've been poor ol' Pete."

"I suspect it was. I saw it, too. Guess we better go back and tell 'em what happened."

"Guess so."

Jack stood. "Ladies, dig out my clothes. Me and Bart's goin' to Colorado. Damn threads'll probably rub my skin raw, it's been so long since I wore any."

Celeste ordered that Pete be released from the wheel, while the other two men prepared for their journey. All gathered in the welcoming room, where Pete proceeded to satisfy any female who hadn't already felt what he was packing.

"Where's Bart's horse?" Jack asked, clutching his trusty Henry repeating rifle and fully outfitted in the same clothes he'd worn when captured.

"Just inside Jacob's hole," answered Celeste. This was the original entrance to the cave, found by Jacob Nehi and closed by his followers once every person and their wagons were safely inside. To get there, Jack and Bart would climb down from their hole of capture and walk a quarter mile east, where the 10-feet-high opening recessed into rock about eight yards. "Been fed and watered. There's one for you, too. Pack horse he brought with him. Elizabeth's watching both." Celeste had sent Elizabeth to fetch the animals after Jack dragged Bart through the hole, figuring it better to give them shelter rather than let them starve to death or fall prey to carnivores.

"Ok, darling, I'll leave it with you. Should be about five days. I'll make sure Mr. Conroy gets his story straight. If I ain't back, go ahead without me. Pete can handle about anything, with or without me."

They looked over to see Pete lying on his back with hands folded under his head for a pillow. Females surrounded him. They one at a time were mounting their steed's mighty cock, riding him like there was no tomorrow.

"Yes, Jack," Celeste grinned. "I think Pete can handle anything or anyone just fine."

"Pete," he yelled, "I'll see ya when I get back."

"Ok." He seemed oblivious to everything except the fuck, but then thought to ask, "Hey, Jack, how long does this stuff work? My dick ain't ever been hard this long."

"Hell, son, I don't know. Guess you can just keep on fornicatin' forever till you get worn out."

"Fine by me," and he returned to his duties. Wasn't a bad idea, he thought. Not a bad life for an escaped convict living in a cave, hidden from the outside world, fed, tended to and fucked for the rest of your days by a gaggle of horny females, but Celeste had other plans for Pete Radcliffe. She'd allow him to satiate the appetites of her daughters, then prepare this man for the future - his very worthwhile future.

"We are Mormons," she told him on the third day of Jack's absence, when Pete's craving for sex had finally subsided enough so that he'd listen to anything not related to the subject of fucking. "Jacob and I broke away when Brigham decided to attack those settlers. Killing innocents has nothing to do with our faith. Jacob brought us all here to continue the true teachings of Joseph Smith."

Of course, Pete didn't have a clue as to what she was talking about - hadn't even heard of the massacre of settlers passing through Utah territory on their way further west. But he sat and listened with respect.

"When we discovered the power of that grey muck in the pool, Jacob knew that was his calling. His duty to god was to right the wrongs of this wild country, but Jacob up and died on me before we could get started. When we stumbled upon Jack, I thought he'd be the perfect man, but he had no sperm. It won't work without semen, Pete."

"What won't work?"

"That grey liquid. It's a truth serum, but it only works when it's fired from the penis of a virile man."

"So, I guess I'm that man."

"To me, you're an incredible man without the serum. When it's in your belly, no gun can harm you, no villain can match your strength. With the serum, you, dear Pete, are invincible."

Jack Hutch did return on that fifth day, and I suppose you'll think me a genuine cad for leaving things as they are right here. But hell, what am I supposed to do? Sit here and write ten books all at once?

Pete and Jack truly did become crime-fighters of the American West. Their many adventures entail sagas of defending the downtrodden and rescuing those in peril. Pete and Jack also, together or solo, often fell into the clutches of evil men and evil women, suffered through interrogations and tortures, but always won the day with their amazing strength and sexual prowess. And all because of that amazing discovery in Jacob Nehi's cave - grey gunk that smelled to high heaven. Sure, it could burn the hairs right out of a man's nostrils, but it also served as truth serum to those who'd done wrong, and as protector of right-minded, horny men.

And so, yes, now that you know how Pete came to be a he-man I must end his beginning, but he will emerge from his cave some day, when I get around to unsealing what Jacob Nehi closed. Look for him along with Jack Hutch, and together we will relive the wild escapades of…

Pete Radcliffe, He-man of the American West

Fem Fist Books

The Boris Bowl
Part 1 - On the Road to Super Sunday

"Oh, look honey, your team scored a touchdown. I guess I'll have to give you a little taste. No, wait, that's the other team. Sorry, it's not my fault your guys are no good."

Pity poor Boris. Not only was he being denied the chance to watch his favorite team play for the National Football League's biggest prize, he also was being denied the chance to release his pressurized nuts of their ever-increasing quantity of sperm. But it was a lesson he had to learn, and one he would never forget.

We'll get back to the game later, but what you should know is that Marsha Palfry adored her husband, nearly to the point of worshiping him. And Boris adored her as well, so the problem came about not from the emotions felt between them, but from the inability, or unwillingness, to express those emotions.

Boris was her first spouse and she was his second. His divorce of number one had left him scarred - from 14 years of once-a-week visits with a child who had been taught to despise him; from endless scorn of a domineering woman, administered by way of harassing telephone calls, letters and gossip spread amongst their circle of friends past and present; from a replacement husband, whose constant verbal challenges to the ex-husband's manhood and invitations to do physical battle tested the nerves, because even though Boris knew he could crush the skinny punk-ass like a cockroach under foot, he also knew any form of accepting these challenges would land them all back in court to revisit terms of the divorce and custody.

It was Marsha who had helped him struggle through these last five years of torment, and although he was the perfect provider in terms of money and whatever material needs she might have, the bedroom was a different matter. Here, those emotional scars interfered. Boris Palfry was unwilling to give all of himself to her, fearful of the vulnerability she so desired of him. She yearned to admire, worship and reward his manhood, but was thwarted in every attempt to do so, until their love-making deteriorated to a man-on-top, under-covers-with-lights-out deposit from penis to vagina. She had become nothing more than toilet water spread on their mattress to receive his discharge.

His was the perfect male form, at least in her mind, and Marsha knew it from the moment they met. Introduced by Brian, their mutual friend, she nearly melted when she saw him, and by the time Boris pecked her cheek with a good night kiss, then saw her safely into the apartment before leaving in a gentlemanly manner, she was overjoyed, knowing that 15 years of waiting for the right man had come to fruition.

And she was right, at least in the beginning of their marriage, but the past few months had shown a new Boris emerging - a domineering, belligerent Boris, who more and more seemed to fancy his wife as some sort of servant, put there to jump at his orders. "Get me a beer," he would bellow. "I'm hungry... fix me a sandwich; This coffee's weak... make another pot; The bathroom stinks... clean it."

Unacceptable behavior without question, but Marsha took it without protest. Rather than confrontation, she chose to allow him these aggressions, not because she feared him, but because she couldn't stand the thought of hurting him. She would not have that on her conscious. This sacrifice became a bubbling cauldron beneath the surface, until in desperation she sought advice from someone who should know, Brian Shields, the very man who had introduced them in the first place.

"Oh, hell, Marsha," he said when she telephoned him at his work, "you know what he's been through. He's just playing the bad ass because he's never been able to before."

"Yeah, well, I've about had my fill of it."

"Is he still in Fresno?"

"Yes, he said it'll take a couple of days to repair the main line."

"Ok, I'll come by the house after my shift ends. Wanna fix me dinner?"

"Sure. What time?"

"Sevenish."

"That will work. See you."

Both men had worked for the railroad since graduating high school. Hired on as apprentice conductors, their employment started in the yards, where they learned to switch, make and break down trains. This also is where the friendship began. From there, Brian became a dispatcher, working in the communication towers to direct trains and crews to their proper assignments. Boris rose to level of crew chief for track maintenance, which would require him to travel when lines were damaged from either natural disasters or railroad accidents.

A derailment in Fresno is what had caused him to be away when Brian knocked on the door of their home. As the avowed bachelor enjoyed a home-cooked meal, Marsha spilled the history of Boris's ever-increasing verbal abuse towards her, sometimes crying, but for the most part nearly shouting, as weeks of pent-up rage were released.

He was a good listener, and when it was clear she had exhausted herself Brian finagled her towards his remedy.

"Boris is pig-headed, Marsha. He's been that way as long as I've known him. I told him a hundred times about that woman. She was bad news. I could see it, but he couldn't. All he could see was that juicy twat between her legs. And believe you me, as soon as she had him hitched up and legal, she led him around like a whipped dog, using that pussy of hers for a leash."

"I know all of that, Brian," she sighed with exasperation, while clearing the table of dirty dishes. "But, hell, it's not my fault. Why's he treating *me* like shit?"

"Because he can. For the first time in years, he suddenly realizes he can throw his weight around and get away with it. That's because you *let* him get away with it."

"Damn," Marsha cupped both hands over her face to fight back tears, "I love him so much. I don't want to cross him, but he won't let me near him at all. Not anymore."

"Maybe a little crossing is what he needs."

"I could never hurt him, Brian, if that's what you mean."

"It's not about hurting him. It's about helping. Problem is, he doesn't realize he's hurting you. So, he needs to learn that there are consequences for his actions. He should be taught how to appreciate his good fortune, which means *you*."

Marsha's resistance slowly faded to curiosity, then intrigue, as Brian made his suggestions for repair. By the time he'd finished with the spicy details, she was tingling with excitement and training session number one took place that very evening. Marsha Palfry and Brian Shields traveled quickly down the road to saving their best friend's marriage.

Part 2 - Pre-Game Hype

"Holy crap, Boris, the Chargers are going to the Super Bowl."

Boris reached over the arm of the couch to give him a high-five, "Un-fucking-believable, first time ever. Marsha, two more beers. Me and Brian's got an AFC Championship to celebrate."

This had been the two men's passion, to huddle before the television set every week during the season to watch their beloved San Diego Chargers. Of course, all of that had ended with Boris's first marriage, but after a six-year interruption, the tradition had been renewed - and continued with wife Marsha, she being a bit more tolerant of man things taking place in her home.

"Ok, buddy, in two weeks, my place."

"Can I come?" Marsha sat down two cans for the boys.

"Sure," Brian smiled and winked, "the more the merrier."

"Oh, shit no, you ain't coming." Boris popped open the can, aiming it towards his wife in hopes of splattering her clothes with a few flying droplets. "You don't want to be around his place. It's a pig sty. For men only."

Marsha sat in a nearby chair and dropped her head, pretending to be hurt, while waiting for Brian to fix the problem.

"Hell, Boris, Marsha doesn't care about that. And besides, we'll need someone to wait on us. Don't want to miss any of the action, right?"

He glared at her, as she sat there looking dejected, then Boris spoke to his pal, "I guess she could be useful."

After slamming down the can of beer, purposefully missing a coaster she had placed on the table, he growled, "Marsha, look at me." She raised her head. "You can come, but you better not speak unless we ask you. I don't want any distractions. And you sure as hell better not walk in front of that TV screen. Understood?"

"Ok, honey."

The franchise known as the Chargers moved from Los Angeles to San Diego, California in 1961, and although they won the American Football League championship three years after that, nobody remembered or cared. That was before the merger with the NFL, before Lamar Hunt had concocted the idea of a "Super Bowl". 33 years later, they had finally made it all the way to the title game. This was important, and so, an all-day event.

Boris and Marsha knocked on Brian's door around 11 am - he with two 12-packs of beer, she with two sacks full of finger food - three hours before game time, three hours of pre-game hype. While the boys watched the interviews and analysis, bitching about what they perceived to be media bias towards the favored San Francisco 49ers, Marsha puttered in the kitchen, filling orders shouted by her husband and occasionally joining them to silently feign interest in the broadcast. She carefully chose a seat closest to the kitchen, so as not to risk blocking the television screen when errands were requested of her.

The last beer for Boris, that being the sedative-spiked beer, was served during the singing of the National Anthem, so that by the time San Francisco was closing in to score their first touchdown, a mere three minutes into the game clock, his eyelids were like anvils.

"Damn, Brian, I'm tired as hell," he sat up in his chair, struggling to stay awake. "I can't... keep my eyes open."

Brian looked at Marsha, then smiled. "Biggest game ever, man. Are you drunk or something?"

"No... no... it's not that. Maybe... a little nap... I just... need a... ..."

Boris could hear the football broadcast when he awoke, but found himself far removed from that comfortable chair. They had draped him face up along the length of a flat, 18-inch high bench, one which Brian normally used for weightlifting. His head rested at one end of the cushioned surface, while the legs were split wide and pulled taut on either side of the lower-middle. With heels resting on the floor, each of Boris's ankles were wrapped in rope, the opposite ends of which ran about 10 feet along the floor, ending at a couch against the wall opposite the television. Here the ropes were knotted to front feet of the couch, one furthest left and the other furthest right. Pulled tightly, the ropes held his legs bound in a downward, V-shaped stretch.

The wrists were also looped in rope, with each end trailing in opposite directions to circle behind a heavy, solid wood cabinet housing the TV and other electronics. Boris's arms were flared with elbows nearly straight and the wrists, four feet apart, were pulled down to a level midway between the floor and bench. This combination of shoulders and arms also formed a V shape, while the chest was forced high into the air, thus flattening and stretching the middle-section.

So, the overall appearance was that of a man on an alter, stretched like the letter X, everything from head to buttocks atop the surface, everything else below. And one final note: every thread of the man's clothing had been stripped away.

Recognizing his confines to be Brian's living room, Boris strained the neck to satisfy his primary subject of curiosity - the game score: San Francisco 7, San Diego 0. The bench had been placed perpendicular to the television screen, with the head of Boris four feet away. After his tortured glance there, he scanned his surroundings. On the floor lay an arsenal of hardware - metal clips, hooks and rings, a roll of duct tape, some sort of walkie-talkie or remote-control device, plastic bottles and a few unidentifiable items, the purpose of which he could not guess.

First, he tested the wrist restraints to find he could move his arms a few inches left or right, but zero inches in any other direction. Next came the legs, which he tried to draw nearer to his torso, the result being no movement of the couch whatsoever. So, he tried to lift upwards, but despite his powerfully-built frame, the result was the same. All he could accomplish was a one-inch rise of his heels from the floor, taking what little slack existed from the two ropes.

As Boris continued to struggle, he heard the voice of his wife, "Look at those flexing muscles, Brian. Isn't he the most beautiful sight you've ever seen?"

Standing at the kitchen doorway were Marsha and Brian, both naked, except for a chain-link collar fastened tightly around the man's neck. Tied into a slip-knot, the chain looped through itself just below his Adam's apple, then the free end trailed to Marsha's hand, which she used to violently jerk downward and repeat her question, "Answer me. Isn't he beautiful?"

Jolted, Brian immediately fell to his knees and obeyed, "Yes, Madam. He is a very beautiful man. Please don't hurt me again."

"Heel, dog. Do what I say. Don't make me waste any more energy on *you.*"

"Marsha," Boris shouted in stunned disbelief, "what the hell are you doing? Untie these ropes."

"Oh, honey, I can't untie you. Those are Brian's knots. I don't know anything about it."

"God damn it! Let me off this thing. We've got to see this game."

"Screw you and your asinine game," she yanked the chain, forcing Brian to an erect knee-stand, hands clutching the neck chain. "Those losers don't have a chance anyway. You can hear it, can't you? They're already getting their ass kicked."

"You crazy bitch." He strained with all his might to break free. "Brian, do something. Marsha's flipped out on us."

She pulled the leash and moved towards her prisoner, forcing Brian to crawl and follow. "Brian can't do shit. He's here to serve me. He'll do whatever I say for a taste of this pussy. By the time I'm finished, neither of you will be the least bit concerned with that fucking game."

Boris gallantly struggled against his bindings. "I'll strangle you first chance I get. Do you hear me? Let me go, NOW!"

Standing confidently beside the bench, she gave another yank of the chain, "Here, boy, it's time to shut his god damn mouth."

Brian dutifully picked up the roll of duct tape he had placed on the floor, tore off a strip and brought it towards the prisoner's face. To avoid this, Boris violently turned his head side to side, until Marsha was forced to secure him between her hands. "Can't you do anything right? There, now slap it on there."

With lips sealed, Boris's attempts at protest were garbled, and so abandoned as useless. Meanwhile, Marsha resumed her taunting. "Don't fret, honey. I won't let Brian hurt you. I'm your super bowl, now." She lifted one leg over him and straddled the bench, leaving her fur-framed cunt to hover above his bulging eyes, then she yanked Brian down to kneel between her husband's head and the TV. "Stay right there, Fido."

With her slave motionless, she dropped the trailing chain from her hand and allowed it to fall to the floor, where it hung against the man's chest and belly. Moving behind him, she took Brian's left wrist into her hand and bent the elbow, placing his hand onto the small of his back. "Don't move," she ordered, while repeating the process with his right hand to leave that forearm stacked above the left.

Grabbing the free end of chain, she pulled it between his legs and yanked hard, which brought pleading from her servant. "Ow, Madam, please, the chain is so tight. It's crushing my nuts."

"Shut it, you cur mutt," Marsha growled, as she kept the chain taut and brought it up through his butt crack towards the forearms. After grabbing a nearby D-ring, Marsha looped the chain around the forearms and wrists repeatedly, using all of the length to keep everything tight. "You'll take what I give you and like it." She locked the chain to itself with D-ring through four links, thus completing his restraint.

Brian dropped his head and bent forward, giving slack to the chain and relief to his scrotum, but was violently jerked backwards, as Marsha grabbed the links behind his neck. Immediately, the back arched and chest thrust forward, which again tightened the chain around his neck and under the balls.

"Do not move an inch," she sneered. "Do it again and I'll crush your gonads with my very own hands. I'll crush them like jelly. Got it, bitch?"

"Yes, Madam, I'll be good. Just don't hurt me."

"I'll do as I please and you can shut your trap. Only speak when I tell you.

Otherwise, I'll slap some tape on your pussy mouth, too."

Silent, her servant was motionless, chest thrust forward and belly sucked in, as Madam Palfry once again straddled her husband and faced the television screen. Placing both palms onto his chest to steady herself, she brought up her legs one at a time and placed the knees into his flat, tight abdominal muscles.

"Now, Boris Palfry," she mocked, "lately you seem to think you can treat me like a pile of horse manure. Do you think I married you so I could be your personal slave? Jumping every time you bark? Waiting on you hand and foot? Night and day?"

There was no attempt to answer, but there was a slight groan, especially when Marsha ground her kneecaps back and forth into his hard belly.

"Well, I can tell you I did not," she answered for him. "And beginning right now, you will learn to show me some respect."

Boris laid there dumbfounded. Just beyond his head was the defeated Brian, his long-time friend, bound with a single chain running from the neck, down the center of chest and belly, under the scrotum and up to locked-behind-the-back arms. Above him, his once-inferior and obedient wife, glaring down with menacing cruelty, while ruthlessly knee-impaling his belly to pulp. And in the background, the play-by-play man announced, "4th and 8, the Chargers will have to punt."

"Of course," she sneered, "they'll be doing that all day." She removed the knees and stood to straddle his chest. Placing the hands onto her own nipples, she delicately rubbed and squeezed, then slid the palms down her middle section to touch the vagina. She widened the opening and invited him to observe. "Look, honey. Would you like to stir this super bowl? Stir it with that big dick of yours? The one you never let me see? Or touch? Or taste?"

Glancing behind her, the husband's penis laid limp, so she plopped down to sit on his chest, then resumed rubbing her own nipples. "Since you don't seem interested, perhaps dog-boy might like a taste. Would that turn you on, darling? To see your buddy molest your wife?"

Boris stared in awe, as Madam Palfry's tit massage caused juices to seep out of her spread-open cunt and ooze onto his chest. Further tormenting him, she moved her hips side to side, smearing the lubricant onto his manly hairs, while adding verbal insults along the way. "Look, sweetheart. See what just a little touching does to me? If you'd ever bother to try it yourself, you'd know these things."

Reaching out with her right hand, Marsha grabbed the left nipple of her chained servant, while continuing to stimulate her own. "How about you, Rex? Would you like me to rip off your tit?"

Between finger and thumb, she viciously twisted and pulled the tip towards her, which caused him to lean forward with a whimper. "I told you not to move, cunt." Grabbing a handful of hair behind his head, she forced it back with her left hand, while pulling on the nipple with her right. He reacted with a muted whine, coupled with a slight grunt, but obeyed her order of verbal silence.

"You are the lucky dog. Since my husband has no interest in me, I will allow you to suck on my tits. You better be professional about it, or you'll lose both of yours."

She pulled him forward by the length of chain running down his chest, forced him to stand, then directed his mouth towards her left breast. Gently, he engulfed the erect nipple between his lips and began to suck, soon incorporating his tongue into the action. For Boris, this was a maddening view. His pal's hardened cock bobbed above his forehead. His wife's orb became saliva-slicked. Lips and tongue lovingly caressed and stimulated, while satisfied moans drifted from the female recipient. With a heightened gusto, Brian joined her chorus of audible expressions, slavishly praising the soft-skinned balloon and its ever-hardening tip.

Naturally, Boris felt anger - anger from being bound and helpless, unable to watch his precious football game; anger and disappointment in his wife's vulgar, inexplicable behavior; anger bordering on rage from being forced to witness her self-instigated desecration.

But there also was a somewhat mysterious, yet undeniable emotion slowly dissolving the first, and that was a yearning - a yearning to break free of his ropes and become a participant, rather than a witness; a desire to lay his own mouth and his own tongue onto her tempting breasts; a longing to unleash his own mighty cock to, in Marsha's words, "stir this super bowl".

He did not realize it when the penis came to life. Blood filled the spongy tissues inside its walls and forced the phallus to rise, then flip onto his flattened belly. The subtle smack of skin touching skin did not escape Marsha's attention, and she spun around to confirm it. Success! A manly tool worthy of his manly physique was aching to join the action. She reached back and clutched her husband's cock into curled fingers, gently squeezing, before updating him on the football game. "Oh, look honey, your team scored a touchdown. I guess I'll have to give you a little taste. No, wait, that's the other team. Sorry, it's not my fault your guys are no good."

14 to 0, still in the first quarter, a long ordeal for Charger fans was well under way.

"Wire him up."

Marsha remained seated on her husband's chest, while slave-boy Brian removed his mouth from her tit. Following the Madam's wishes, he retrieved a ring made of rubber, carefully slipping it over the cock shaft, then around and under the ball sac. On the outer surface of the ring at opposite sides were two tiny, metal pins - receptors, and after Brian handed a battery-operated remote device to Ms. Palfry, she turned a dial, sending a small electrical current throughout the innards of the cock ring. A gentle vibration enlivened cock and balls.

The prisoner's eyes widened, beads of sweat broke onto his forehead, as his wife's tender, yet near-psychotic gaze mystified him. What were the intentions? Was she truly angry, to the point of inflicting serious damage? Or was it merely a game, a form of pretend punishment designed to please her? And why was Brian only putting up a half-assed resistance? Unable to verbalize his concerns, with no "safe" or "out" words given to him, Boris was forced to trust that his captors knew what they were doing. He only hoped.

Tingling vibrations encompassed an ever-hardening penis. Bulbous balls ballooned. Manly groans rumbled underneath duct tape. Another notch turned on the dial caused the chest to expand, back to arch, belly to flatten and pelvis to thrust upwards. Boris Palfry, fully charged both in mind and body, launched his mighty cock high into the air and reached for the unreachable.

She slid her ass to the end of his sternum, passed the remote to Brian, and delicately fingernail-flicked his nipple tips. "Boris, honey," she lightly scraped the stretched tits with nails, "you probably didn't hear it, but the Chargers got a touchdown. Are you happy?"

A muffled "Mmm" and nod of the head was his reply.

"Your man-tits make me drip," she opened the right one between finger and thumb, then covered it with her mouth, sucking and massaging with lips and tongue. Releasing it, she wet-rubbed the tip with her finger. "Are you still happy?"

A Neanderthal-sounding "Ungh" rumbled under duct tape.

Sharp-edged nails pressed down onto the erect tips of his nipples. A manly groan. More beads of forehead sweat. "Did I ever tell you how much I love your nose?" She raised into a squat and inched forward. "Sculptured, strong," the salivating clit dangled above his face, "just like you, just like all of you." She dropped the wedge onto his covered mouth, ramming her juicy cunt into his nostrils. "Breathe, darling. You deserve this. Suck with all your strength."

He lustfully inhaled her, first from want, then for oxygen, very little of which was allowed. An inch was given and he recovered, then again was smothered, as the majestic nose disappeared into a sizzling cut of fur-lined filet.

"Come here, slave," she summoned the collared one.

Once within reach, she grabbed the chain trailing down his chest and forced him to kneel at the head-end of the bench. "This is for you, cur, not him." Lifting her hips to reposition, the green light was given, "Now, feast."

With his wife's aromatic ass rim hovering inches above his nose, the prisoner was forced to watch the slave eat pussy. A wet tongue expertly teased the hooded cover, then delved into its pulsating meat. Probing deeper, a gradual intensity produced a frothing combo - male, oral spit, female, vaginal slickum - a heavenly mixture dripping into the burning eyes of a man tormented.

He now was fully aware of his neglected cock, gyrating with electrically-charged energy, lustfully bouncing on his belly with each accelerated heartbeat. Lubricant of his own making splattered onto tightened, writhing abdominal muscles, darkening the fur trail with beads of syrup.

Sounds stimulated. Slurping suction, moans of ecstasy - high-pitched, low-pitched - echoed from ceiling and walls, usurping whatever drivel beamed from the nearby boob tube. Female hands cupped female breasts. Fingers and thumbs pinched hardened tips. Pre-orgasmic shrieks crescendoed, then were silenced, as Madam P clutched the dog-collar chain to viciously cast her lover aside, "Well done, whore. Now, get out of my sight."

Taking the remote from him, she stepped away from the bench to absorb a glorious side-view of her bound prisoner. Writhing, flexing, thrusting into nothingness, his agony only further heightened the intense pressure building in her loins. She longed to mount him - to finish him; to finish herself, but all such thoughts were to be squashed. Unknown heights of pleasure were yet to be explored, and the bladder reminded her that other issues should be addressed. Madam P turned the dial to zero and set the remote on the floor.

"I see that it's halftime and I *will* be watching the festivities. The score is Niners 28, Chargers 7. Your situation seems hopeless, but relax, my darling. Perhaps you can mount a comeback."

She met Brian as he exited the bathroom and they conversed out of character.

"God, Brian, this is so much fun."

"How's he doing?"

"Looks ok to me. I turned off the voltage, so you better get the bottle and let him piss."

She closed the door and emptied her own bladder, too.

Part 3 - Second-half Blowout

As Brian removed the urine-filled bottle from a mostly faded penis, Marsha brought a chair from the kitchen table, positioned it to the right of her husband's chest, and sat facing the television. In her left hand, the cock ring controller; in her right, a bottle of isopropyl alcohol. "Bet you really had to pee, huh?" He nodded. "Would you like another beer?" He nodded. "Well, I suppose you can have... Oh, look, honey, there's Patti LaBelle. I just love her."

Boris Palfry did not strain to look, instead turning his head away in frustration. Nor did he bother to look when he felt a wet finger touch his right nipple. He had seen the bottle and knew its contents were harmless, but what he did not know was the effect it would have on the stretched and sensitive knob. After an initial burn, a stinging coolness caused the skin to contract, forcing the tip to elevate well above his chest. A layer to the left nipple was followed by a second one to the right, and a finger gently rubbed the liquid in small circles.

Turning the dial to number one, she laid the remote onto the center of his downward-sloping stomach, and he raised the head to witness another brutal assault on his defenseless tits. Boris was confronted with a new dilemma. His nipples were responding to the stinging of alcohol and massaging of fingers. Outside, the circles expanded from heat, then shrank from cold. Inside, amazing sensations of masculine power overwhelmed, causing him to feel as though he were some sort of manly hero. Lowering the head, he felt the ropes binding his wrists and pulled against them - not to escape, but to flex, pose and display his incredible physique. Boris had never fancied himself to be such a man, but this assault on his nipples seemed to be changing his attitude. More convincing was soon to come.

"Hey, you," Marsha barked to her servant, just arrived from dumping the urine bottle, "put some on his nuts." He approached and she removed the D-ring, unwrapping the chain to release his arms, but as he reached for the alcohol, Brian was greeted with a backhanded slap to the cheek. "Not mine, you moron. Get another bottle. And keep quiet. Tony Bennett's about to perform."

The prisoner's cock was quickly resurrected. A one-notch turn of the dial caused it to majestically rise, slide along the thigh and rest in the crook between leg and pelvic bone. Fresh coats of alcohol onto finger-massaged tits completed the ascent, as an involuntary scrotum clinch launched it into the air. Relaxing the clinch brought it slamming down onto the belly. An initial layer onto the testicles, compliments of Brian, caused the pulsating tool to dance upon flattened muscle, leaving dots of slick discharge with each contact.

Burning, stinging, cooling, the alcohol attacked both nipples and nuts, transporting the bound hero into a fantasy land. His head lifted. He admired his own glorious form. Real restraints dramatized the image of pretend torture. Testosterone raged throughout his bloodstream, as he struggled against the ropes, flexing himself in a mighty pose of resolve.

He gave no forethought to what was happening. They had taken him to a place of exploration, a place maddeningly exciting. With no intention of leaving, his mind joined the body in participation.

Beneath the tape, his lips mumbled manly expressions of defiance. "Damn sons-a-bitches, think you can break me. I'm too much man for both of you."

Marsha could see, feel and hear what was happening. The protective walls her husband had built for himself were crumbling, and she prepared to complete the demolition.

"Halftime is over." She stepped towards the television, pressed the power off, and glared at Boris. "So is the football game, as far as you're concerned. Your contest is with me now, tough guy."

To the collared servant she growled, "Wet those nuts every 30 seconds, if you can count that far."

Lifting the remote from her bound prisoner's stomach, she turned the dial to three and set it on the bench near its foot end. Her servant, who was straddling the bench near Boris's knees and bent forward towards the target, continued to transfer stimulating liquid from fingers to nuts, carefully painting the swollen orbs on top, bottom, underneath and in between. Isolated and lifted by the vibrating ring, the testicles surpassed human qualities, appearing to Brian as the balls of a mighty bull - vibrant, full of life, full of impatiently waiting sperm.

A manly groan accompanied a pelvic thrust. The fully-hardened cock stood, suspended in mid-air, suspended in time, seconds counted by the Madam... 7... 8... 9... 10, until finally, the electrified tool collapsed onto his belly, only to react from contact of corona to muscle, thus rising to begin the count anew.

For Marsha, a dramatic side-view brought salivation between jaws and thighs. Her hero strained against the wrist-binding ropes. Fists clenched. Chest expanded. Nipple tips pierced the air, while exaggerated exhales flattened the belly. Massive thighs exploded. Sinewy calf ligaments contorted. Manly feet undulated - toes curling forward, toes arching backward, and all the while, he stared at her with eyes lustful, yearning, begging, the expressions so long denied her, the emotions so long concealed, finally stripped and laid bare.

Sweat - glistening, masculine sweat, highlighted every line, every curve, every bulge of his body, and the language it spoke tempted her, inviting her to ravage. She knelt beside the flexing belly and heaving chest. She listened to each release of air. She heard deep-toned, guttural, cave-man grunts. The dominant male demanded his woman, but was powerless to take her.

"Why do you make me torture you?" The right hand slid under his cock head to deep-massage the brick-wall belly. "No one wants you to suffer this way." The left hand lay flat on his chest, moving side to side, savagely rubbing the erect nipples. "I can't bear to see you like this." Lips pressed his stomach, planting kisses. "You are so strong." Tongue tasted his sweat. "Such a man." Nose inhaled his musk. "I will worship you like a god. I will put you on a pedestal, the manliest man ever to grace the earth."

Into her fist she clutched his cock shaft, lifting it to vertical. Out of the tube came masculine paste, which oozed from the slit to coat its mushroom head.

"Hold this," she ordered. "Hold it in your mouth."

The servant wrapped wet lips over the bulging cock head, stopping at the umbrella-like rim extending from the shaft. In response, Boris convulsed and tried to thrust his pelvis upwards, but was thwarted by the wife's hands, which were firmly planted into his belly.

"Clamp it tightly," she whispered," but don't work it. If you make him shoot, I will castrate you. Do you hear me? I will literally remove your dangling balls. Cut them and eat them."

With curved fingers, she manipulated the hard-muscled abdominals. Her victim arched his back, tightening the middle, then dramatically exhaled, relaxing the middle. She heard him groan, saw him strain the legs - not to pull them together, but to push them apart, begging for a resumption of testicle torture.

Again with a whisper Marsha ordered, "Layer his 'nads."

Her hero raised the head when he felt renewed stinging on his nuts, first looking to her, then to his cock, its mushroom hidden by the lips of his best friend. The idea of having a man's mouth upon his penis might have caused apprehension under normal circumstances. The idea that Brian might be capable of such an act had never occurred to him. This circumstance was far from normal, and considering where he had been and where he was going, neither fact was given a thought. With an ecstatic, upward roll of the eyes, followed by a muted, agonizingly long and breath-released, "Uuunnngghhh", Boris collapsed. He was surrendered, willing to accept anything they wanted to give him.

The moment for which she had so long waited had arrived. Her eyes locked onto it, trance-like. Inhaling caused it to become thick, solid, impenetrable. Exhaling caused it to explode with powerful lines and curves. A singular, deep ridge formed at the pit of the stomach, ran to the navel and disappeared beneath one line of narrow, then widening man fur.

Into this heaven she buried her face. On the surface, soft and cushioned, but just beneath was a wall of concrete, a bunker of protection. Breathing through her mouth, she pressed down harder, and harder, but the barrier could not be broken. Here was the ultimate definition of masculine strength. Here was nothing but muscle, no bone to protect the innards. Here was the apex of a man's vulnerability, for regardless of whatever fat might be collected and stored there, the muscle underneath, when tensed, was masterfully designed to protect him from any assault. To surrender it, to offer it up to the whims of another, this is the pinnacle of trust.

Her man, her husband, gave her this gift. His belly was 100 percent rock-solid, but she felt it give way beneath her. She thanked him for her gift with kisses - not delicate kisses, but deep, penetrating, face-burying kisses. Every inch was attacked, from the pit of the stomach to the belly button and beyond. From the pubic hair, she began her return to the stomach with tongue licks - not dry, tip-of-the-tongue licks, but full-appendage, loaded with spit, sliming licks. She tasted and removed his sweat, while leaving behind her saliva.

And then she came to the center of it all - *his* super bowl. Where life itself had begun. The knot. The place where momma fed him before he left that world of darkness. The doctor had tied his knot so you could see it. The rim of his belly button framed what was, in Marsha's mind, the most beautiful gob of skin she could ever imagine. It laid ever so slightly beneath the belly itself, clearly visible and readily available. Her tongue teased, first moistening the edged rim, then moving like a whirlpool, round and round and gradually down, finding its way to his belly button. She wet-scraped its surface, then used the tip of her tongue to drill him a new hole. Streams of spit ran down her tongue and into this hole, spilling over the rim to flow in all directions, tributaries forming on the belly's surface.

Marsha knew she had tamed him. Her belly button worship brought painfully pleasured moans each time he exhaled. And, as further proof, these air releases seemed to last forever. After breathing out, he'd hold position and force his belly to remain in its most flattened, most vulnerable stature, while the woman's tongue mercilessly impaled the knotted navel.

Brian also knew. He watched the belly attack in amazement, while he continued to alcohol rub the testicles. In his mouth, the man's penis swelled to incredible strength. A constant buzz came from the cock ring at its base, but at the head, where Brian's lips held firm, rippling reverberations exploded. Pulses of power coinciding with each heartbeat pounded on Brian's oral vise, triggered by the slavish worship of a woman's tongue. He dared not move. Any added stimulation would push their hero over the edge, and Brian had no desire to receive the man's seed. That was reserved for Marsha - the only reason for any of this.

Clutching the shaft of her husband's cock, she motioned for Brian to release him, then laid the surging man-tool onto a glistening-with-spit belly. "Stay still." She took his dangling chain and stood. "Come with me." With a gentle tug of chain, she guided him to the end of the bench, then whispered, "Get down there and lick his foot."

Stepping over the bench, she straddled and smothered her victim's writhing torso. His cock was wedged between titties; the gut assaulted by lips, face and tongue; his chest and nipples ravaged by palms, fingers and nails. She undulated towards his contorting face, sliding inch by inch, mixing his sweat with hers. Hardened breasts scraped along his dramatic, sloping abdomen, as her stomach crushed his tortured cock head. Climbing the mountain, her tits reached the mighty chest. That salivating pussy hole lingered atop the phallic masterpiece, then moved onward to further slime his stomach. Hands and fingers clutched his hair and massaged the scalp, while lips and tongue moved from one tormented nipple to the other, kissing, sucking, licking.

Breathless, she sat upright, clamping his chest between thighs. The man beneath her, the pitiful, tortured soul, desperately lifted his head, straining to bury an anguished face into that tantalizing V, so close, yet so out of reach.

"You are mine, Boris Palfry," she lifted off of him and maneuvered her twat above his head. "You are mine forever," she violently ripped the tape from his mouth and replaced it with pussy. "I'm never letting you go. You belong to me. Understand?"

Garbled agreement intermingled with thirst-quenching slurps.

"Only I can give you what you must have."

His lips encompassed the top and bottom of her vaginal slit, while the tongue snaked its way into darkness, searching for the little G, the vibrating peter, his prize.

"You are a god to me. I must worship, but you must sacrifice all. I will have every inch of you, or I will have none of you."

Non-verbal acceptance came from below. His mouth could only express a gurgling, "Mmm hmm," as he frantically choked on tasty juices.

Her body shuddered when the tongue made contact with that heavenly spot. Her voice squeaked when its wet-sandpapered surface scraped what it had found. But this was not the orgasm she had worked so hard to achieve. She stood, denying both herself and him.

Finally able to speak, Boris said nothing - nor did Marsha, nor did Brian. Physical expressions circumvented all talk.

Brian dutifully slimed the right foot and its toes. Marsha joined in on the left foot. Not knowing or caring who was worshiping which, the hypnotized man arched back all toes and spread them wide, sacrificing his masculine feet to this incredible praise. The tongues visited thick-skinned soles, racing upon strong arches, rough heels and rounded ball joints. Exploring further, they slithered in between the great and second toes, oiling the skin with foaming spit before moving between second and third to repeat the assault.

Coinciding with this intense praise of the feet, hands created hot, rubbing friction from knees to ankles, while finger squeezes crushed thick calf muscle. His reaction was a crazed writhing, a torturous arching of the spine to a degree of near-snapping, or so it appeared.

He was rescued by a straddling of the bench. With each hand holding one bottle, she dumped the contents of both, saturating his chest and belly with mesmerizing alcohol. Into her hand, he was held vertical; into her cunt, he was given his reward. She angled the bulging mushroom head to make direct contact with her yearning clitoris, then hugged the thickness of his massive cock. It was a vaginal death clamp, crushing, inhaling. No further action was needed, as both were primed for explosion. Two became one. Milk spewed.

They froze in a statuesque pose - the dominant male beneath, back curved to the maximum his bindings would allow, the praising female above, hands pressed into his tightened belly. Neither participant breathed. Eyes shut, mouths agape, all movement was confined to contracting muscles of sex, until, as if on cue they violently exhaled, emitting animalistic cries of unbridled pleasure. Collapsing, contorting, convulsing, they simultaneously erupted to vanquish all pent-up frustrations, all secretive sadness, to enter a magical world they would never leave. He belonged to her - all of him, and she fell forward to press her lips with his, to flatten her breasts with his, leaving no separation between.

This is the sight that greeted Brian when he stood, his own personal satisfaction, as he absorbed the mesmerizing reunion of this man and this woman. With three strokes of the hand, he spewed his own seed, not caring upon whom or what it landed. He had brought them together in the beginning; he had guided their rediscovery today. With a woman's head resting peacefully on a man's chest, that man's buried penis basking in the loving confines of unyielding devotion, Brian Shields reached down to the bench, turned the dial and moved it to zero.

Super Bowl XXIX was a sad, sad day for many San Diego residents, but not for the Palfry's, nor their best friend. In fact, their Super Bowl party continued into the next morning, transferred from the living room to the bedroom. Without ropes, Boris proved to be that manly god his wife claimed him to be, sacrificing himself to the praise of two, then satisfying both with other-worldly eruptions. Brian was the swing man and oral expert, equally excited to pleasure the cunt of one or cock of the other - and everything in between.

As for the Palfry's together, all was complete. No need for him to give commands - politely or otherwise, because she knew exactly what he needed at all times. And when she was ready, his body was hers. With plenty of light, tied up or no, Boris gladly posed and flexed, spouting dramatic expressions of the tortured hero, before flooding her with everything she desired. All of him, that's what Marsha demanded, and Boris could not be satisfied any other way.

Do not pity poor Boris. He is the happiest man in the world.

Fem Fist Books

The Milking Tree
Part 1 - Wrath of the Natashi

Dr. Richard Cargill was a professor, explorer and treasure hunter. His painstaking research and planning always brought him his prize, and every one of his campaigns had been a success - until this one.

At the moment, Cargill found himself stripped naked and suspended, his wrists roped to tree limb, his arms in parallel lines overhead and toes inches from the ground. His wrist ropes were draped over the limb about 15 feet above the ground, where their length returned to the ground and were tied to a wooden stake driven into the ground.

Under the canopy of this lone tree in the center of a village clearing somewhere in southern Africa, hundreds of miles from nowhere, Cargill helplessly watched the torture and execution of what remained from his expedition: three load-bearers, also stripped naked, bound to wooden poles eight feet in length and standing vertical not more than 10 yards from where Richard Cargill dangled. All four men that very morning had been pounced upon and taken prisoner by a tribe of fierce female warriors known as the Natashi, and now, while waiting and wondering what fate awaited him, Cargill fought the urge to regurgitate from the brutality perpetrated upon his pitiful men.

Each man faced him. Each man hung with wrists crossed behind their poles and tied with rope, while their ankles were bound in the same manner, their feet inches from the ground. Gravity stretched them. Because their limbs were roped behind the poles, their torsos protruded towards Cargill. Because their limbs were crossed, their chests and bellies formed a V shape with rib cages expanded and abdomens flattened. Because their poles were buried in the open without protection overhead, unlike Cargill who was shaded by 60-foot tree, their ebony skin glistened with sweat, the unforgiving late-morning sun baking them with ungodly heat. And for reasons Cargill could not begin to guess, the leader of this Natashi tribe (a woman Cargill privately named Blue-face because of the dazzling designs of blue painted across her high cheekbones) allowed her female warriors to savagely beat these helpless men with wooden clubs.

She shouted a command and her warriors sprang into action. With two Natashi women assigned to each victim, the pairs ruthlessly assaulted these glorious men. Powerful men they were, devoid of fat and bulked with muscle, muscle built naturally from transporting on foot many pounds of cargo hundreds of miles countless times. None of their strength could help them now. Cargill tried not to look, but each horrific impact of blunted wood to stretched torso brought agonizingly horrific grunts and screams. He had to look. They were his men, his companions, his responsibility.

As the female pairs grew weary, Blue-face ordered them to hand their clubs to the next groups of two's and the beatings continued without interruption. The men howled and cried out as their chests and abdomens were viciously pounded to putty. Cargill could hear the unholy cracks and pops of ribs and other bones breaking.

Each warrior had their opportunity to batter their victims, and as the final pairs dropped their clubs in exhaustion, Blue-face stalked up and down the line, inspecting what was left, making sure her sister warriors had done a proper job. Apparently pleased, she with commanding authority ordered the females to begin tearing the men's skin to shreds with whips. Again matched in pairs assigned to each victim, they relentlessly laid their whips across the battered bellies and chests of the pitiful prisoners, following the same pattern as before by passing the whips down the line, until all had been satisfied.

Cargill tried to shut out the unholy screams of agony coming from the poles. Impossible. Their cries permeated the village until he thought his head would explode, and as the lashings ended Cargill stared in disbelief at what remained of his pitiful helpers. Their once gloriously masculine physiques now hung as though slaughtered meat upon vertical poles, sweat and blood intermingling to drip off their toes to the ground below. Screams and pleadings had turned to sobs and moans. One of them seemed to praying, surely for death, as Cargill also prayed for them, for it was he who had led them here to this god-forsaken place, only to see them turned to bloody, battered, living corpses.

His anguish soon turned to shock and amazement. Appearing from one of the huts came a man - a white man who wore nothing but a loin wrapping and some sort of vegetation-made crown upon his head. Three females were knelt in front of the prisoners as the white man hovered nearby. They tied the victims's genitals by use of thin animal hide strips, wrapping them behind the testicles and over the tops of their penises, tightly securing the strips at the base of each. As the women stepped away, each phallus became engorged with blood, as the strips slowed the exiting flow from their dangling male organs.

Now the white man stood before one of the battered men. He knelt on the ground and began performing oral service upon him, which caused the man's body to flex. Despite being half-dead, this hapless victim was forced to respond to the oral assault on his isolated and hardened penis. His face was shrouded with anguish and utter humiliation - anguish from the pain of his brutalized torso - humiliation from the degradation inflicted upon his exposed manhood.

The tempo increased and soon the prisoner shot his load into the tormentor's mouth, as the white man continued sucking on the spent penis to elicit every last drop into his throat and down to his gut. This relentless assault on the sensitive cock forced the prisoner to involuntarily flex and twitch, causing ungodly pain to reverberate throughout his broken and brutalized body.

Then the white man released the organ, rose to his feet and proceeded to the next victim, where he knelt to perform the same task on that man's penis. Cargill watched in horror as his poor men were one by one degraded before the female warriors. The Natashi relished this spectacle. They chirped and chattered. Each twitching of prisoner brought laughter. Each moan of pain and humiliation brought mocking with fingers pointing. They viciously ridiculed what was left of the pitiful wretches stretched before them, as the myterious white man extracted manly fluids from each cock, leaving the cock owners spent and nearly lifeless on their poles of torture.

He now turned and approached the tree, followed closely by Blue-face and the rest of the tribe. Cargill shuddered. Were they coming for him? Was it his turn to suffer what he'd just witnessed? Instead, the man ignored and drifted past him, continuing on until he reached the trunk of the mighty tree. The warriors formed a circle around the trunk behind Cargill and began a solemn chant. Attempting to see what was happening, Cargill peeked over his shoulder and watched in wonder as the white man stuffed his fingers into his throat, gagged himself, and spit what he'd regurgitated onto the trunk of the tree. Man seed, fresh semen taken from three tortured and slowly-dying prisoners, that's what was spit onto the tree.

The she-warriors broke into frenzied celebration, chanting, flailing their arms and dancing in wild circles. As he dropped his head to rest on his chest, Cargill at first was saddened, but then sickened and angered by the spectacle taking place behind him. His poor men had suffered unspeakable tortures, just so these savages could spit sperm onto a goddamn tree. And what was worse, the instigator of these atrocities seemed to be not the savages - which, while not excusable, could at least be somewhat understandable - but rather, it was the white man, perhaps at one time or another a civilized man, who had done this to his fellow human beings. To be sure, this ritual most-likey had been part of Natashi culture since the tribe came into being, but still, the lone male had played a major role, and Cargill vowed to himself that when and if opportunity came to him for exacting revenge, he'd take it. He'd do so not for himself, but for his men.

As the crazed celebration drifted back towards the three prisoners, spears soon pierced their chests and abdomens, finally bringing an end to their unholy suffering. The white man did not participate. Cargill felt the mysterious man's presence behind him, and then heard his voice. "Dr. Cargill, my name is Roger Trout."

Part 2 - The Kutambi Elephant

Cargill's eyes widened upon hearing the name. Roger Trout was known as a famed explorer and treasure hunter like himself, but the name had faded from the memories of most people involved in this field of adventure.

As the story goes, Roger Trout launched an expedition 16 years prior, seeking the same treasure that brought Cargill to Africa. This Roger Trout and all who came with him had not been heard from since, thought lost forever.

Trout smiled as he faced his prisoner, not in a welcoming and brotherly way, but in a sinister and superior way. "I see from the stupid expression on your face that you remember me. Imagine my delight when the scouts told me an expedition had passed through our jungle. I immediately knew what you were looking for. Did you find it?"

Richard Cargill hesitated, knowing the first words he spoke would determine his immediate future. "Find what?"

"Don't insult me doctor. Surely you were looking for the statue, the magnificent Kutambi Elephant... more importantly, the tusks, the two little 10-inch tusks covered with hundreds of the most perfect diamonds ever known to mankind."

"I found nothing. I failed just as you did. It is nothing but a myth. The ruins are still there, but nothing remains of value."

"LIAR!" Trout launched a barrage of punches upon Cargill's defenseless body. He unleashed 16 years of frustration on the poor man. Fists rained into his gut, onto his rib cage and sternum. Cargill grunted and groaned in accepting these blows, flexing all muscles in defense. Slowly circling, Trout continued to pound on him from the back side, targeting his kidneys and shoulder blades before returning to the front of his victim to deliver more blows into his abdomen and chest until exhaustion forced him to rest.

Now both men were gasping for air. After several deep breaths, Trout continued the interrogation. "I went through your clothing. I read the notes on every chart and map you had with you. I saw your log book, doctor. Do you think I'm stupid?"

Still trying to recover from his beating, Cargill knew his game was up but for one piece of the puzzle: the diamonds. He'd written nothing in regards to the tusks. Their location was known only to his memory, and so rather than answer Trout's stupid question about who thought who was stupid, Cargill tried some offense. "What kind of man are you? How could you stand by and let these savages murder those innocent men?"

"None of that is your concern. You are alive and that is all that matters. I read all about your little misadventure. How and where you found the statue. How you lost it when your expedition was obliterated by the stampeding elephants. You mentioned that you left the statue behind on the plain, but what about the tusks? I know you were not foolish enough to leave them behind. Talk to me, Dr. Cargill."

Cargill flexed his chest as he spoke, " I left it all. What else could I do? Only three men were left alive to help me and the tusks were gone. They were crushed into the ground along with the rest of my men and supplies. All we could do was try to survive and return to the coast."

"You are a fool. You saw what happened to your men. Do not force me to let the women have their way with you." Trout resumed pounding his prisoner's torso, shouting one word in between each punch, "You... will... talk...... NOW!"

Cargill tightened every muscle in his helpless body to receive the pounding. He clenched his teeth and threw back his head, not wishing to see the blows rain on him, but this time Trout tired quickly and the beating stopped.

"What you have witnessed here today will pale in comparison to what I have in store for you. For 16 years I have waited for this day. I knew someone would come to seek my treasure. It is MY treasure, you know. I will have it, doctor. You cannot win."

And with that, Roger Trout returned to his hut.

During this little getting to know you between Cargill and Trout, the she-warriors had been busy cutting down the corpses of Cargill's bearers, dragging the carcasses to a seven-foot diameter pit dug into the earth a few yards to his left.

Smoke drifted out of the pit and had been since the entire spectacle started, and this smoke added more misery to the already miserable midday heat. He saw them brandish knives and remove something from the lifeless bodies, but refused to believe what he thought he saw. After all, he couldn't be sure and did not want to think about such a thing. Carcasses were thrown into the pit, becoming fuel for the coals below to create a stench of burning flesh that permeated the entire village, and after Blue-face received from one of her warriors a wooden bowl, she and the rest of her tribe disappeared into their huts, leaving the suspended man to suffer alone under the mighty tree.

Cargill's entire upper body ached. The ropes suspending him burned his wrists, as they were forced to bear all of his weight, while gravity relentlessly stretched him. Although he was protected by shade from the tree and its canopy towering above him, his body was covered with sweat from the noon time heat and foul smoke drifting from the pit of fire. Passing minutes seemed like hours. He thirsted for water, having received no sustenance since his capture, and mercifully, relief came.

Blue-face emerged from her hut and entered another hut nearby, then reappeared and strutted towards the prisoner. Following behind her, three men of the tribe shuffled their feet trying to keep pace with their tribal leader, a stuttered gait caused by the ropes connecting their ankles. One single binding wound around each ankle, connected by a two-foot length in between, thus limiting the size of their steps to this amount. One of the men carried a bucket, as Blue-face stood before Cargill and flashed her teeth to display her fierce superiority. The suspended man had been and still was somewhat in awe of this female, with her bright blue designs highlighting her cheekbones, and short-cropped black hair following the roundness of her head forcing him to remember what she'd done to his men. Otherwise, he risked fantasies that might bring arousal, which might remind her that the tree needed its ritual of prisoner beatings and prisoner semen. Nonetheless, he inspected her with his eyes. Adorned with decorative wooden anklets, the rest of her stood naked. Nothing interrupted her feminine curves and lines of ebony skin, and the beauty of her slender, but muscular legs and buttocks was matched only by her perfectly rounded breasts and commanding face.

She turned to nod at the man with the bucket and he set it down, scooped out a wooden bowl full of water and raised it for Cargill to drink. He voraciously lapped up the precious liquid, so eager to quench his thirst that he didn't notice when Roger Trout joined the group. As the bowl was emptied and lowered, Cargill recognized his own clothes covering Trout, the same attire that the Natashi had stripped from him that very morning.

"Dr. Cargill, I am going to give you the benefit of the doubt. I have studied your notes and plotted a path back to the scene of your mishap." Trout now mocked his prisoner. "You should have known that elephants are very sensitive creatures. They do not like to be disturbed when they are feasting. My, how they do love to strip bark and leaves from the Acacia trees!"

Cargill did not give his tormentor the satisfaction of a response, and so Trout continued. "I estimate my journey to take two hours each direction. I will see for myself if what you say is true. Do not begin to guess what will happen to you if you have tried to deceive me."

After delivering one more punch to Cargill's stomach, he then spoke the language of the Natashi to the three men. Two of them shuffled over to the stake, untied the ropes and lowered the prisoner back to earth. As Cargill collapsed to the ground, the third man cut the ropes from his wrists and immediately placed ankle restraints same as his own onto the prisoner, while the other two lifted Cargill to his feet.

"It is good that your clothes fit me," Trout's sarcastically droned on. "They seem to smell a bit sour. Tell me, is it normal for you to produce this volume of sweat, or did something frighten you?"

Cargill again was silent.

"Enjoy your temporary relief, doctor. In four hours I will return for you."

With Blue-Face joining him as guide and protecter, Roger Trout disappeared into the jungle growth to search for his long-denied treasure.

Part 3 - The Human Pendulum

The three men escorted Cargill towards their hut. He wearily staggered while they shuffled along beside him and supporting him, his body exhausted from hours of torturous suspension, beatings and denial of water. Once inside, he was laid chest down onto a floor mat of tightly woven leaves, where he immediately collapsed into sleep. As he did, the men began washing away the sweat and dirt from his body, but Cargill felt none of this. His mind was dreaming of places far, far away, places of peace and tranquility. The men soothed his body with salves and ointments, applying them with deep muscle massages.

When Cargill awoke he was laying on his back and feeling refreshed but hungry. One of the men offered him a bowl filled with some kind of meat, the odor and texture of which he recognized as snake meat. He filled his belly. As Cargill ate, one of the men verbalized something to him, and using what he had learned from his studies of African cultures Cargill was able to interpret bits and pieces of what the man was saying.

He wanted to know where the white man came from. Using words he knew and hand gestures, Cargill tried to describe his far-away world to the savages. Their wide-eyed smiles confirmed their understanding of what he was telling them, and then Cargill asked them about their lives.

They were born into the tribe as slaves, used only for servitude and reproduction. In their world, females ruled. Only one of ten male infants born to the tribe was allowed to survive, and at present their were no infants either male or female. This was a revelation Cargill had failed to notice when suspended from the tree. For the entirety of their lives this guarded hut had been their dwelling place. They were only allowed to leave it when summoned to perform tasks for the females, usually labor, but sometimes functional sexual intercourse.

Cargill laughed as the man indicated the word "fuck" by inserting his index finger into a circle made with his other hand, but only Blue-face could say when and whom they could fuck. Each man was denied intercourse but for one time every four seasons. Cargill was saddened by the plight of these men. Just imagine it: no pussy for eleven out of every twelve months, and even then, their once-per-year fuck was no more meaningful or emotional than shitting a daily turd. He wondered if they really knew how bad things were for them. He tried to make them understand that, where he came from, men and women were equal, at least that was the goal. Again their excitement over his world showed in their faces, and Cargill began to feel a bond forming amongst the four of them, but this train of thought was interrupted when Trout and Blue-face entered the hut.

"Dr. Cargill, I do not believe your story. The corpses and supplies, even the statue, were clearly visible. The Kutambi Elephant is in my hut right now, but the tusks and diamonds are gone. Where did you take them?"

"Someone beat you to the prize, Trout. I left it all there."

"You take me for a fool, but I assure you that I am not. Soon you will gladly tell me everything I want to know."

Trout and Blue-face stormed out of the hut, and within minutes two she-warriors entered to violently lift Cargill to his feet. They cut the ropes from his ankles and led him back towards the tree, where the entire tribe was gathered and waiting.

A major modification had been made to the suspension apparatus. One rope each was attached to the end of a five-foot log, five inches in diameter. Cargill was positioned facing away from the tree and the log placed on his shoulders. Then his arms were stretched in opposite directions and wrists strapped to the log with strips of animal hide. The ropes were pulled to lift Cargill's arms past his head, until his toes barely touched the ground. Now a log of equal size was brought from behind him. Large rocks had been tied to the top of the log, all of them together weighing 50 pounds. Cargill's feet were spread one foot apart and ankles then strapped to the front of the log. Once again, the ropes were pulled several inches and tied to the stake at the other end, leaving his feet three inches off the ground.

Cargill groaned in pain and humiliation, as he was again suspended naked before the savage females. The weight of the rocks increased his crucifixion stretching, forcing his chest to expand and belly to flatten. Immediately, he struggled to breathe, his diaphragm being hopelessly compressed.

Having again adorned his tribal garb of loin wrap and vegetation crown, Roger Trout joined the gathering with Blue-face standing beside him. "Cargill, this will be a long, torturous evening for you. Your fate will not be a quick, merciful death like those of your companions. No, I will make sure these women take it slow and easy on you. Now, tell me about the diamonds."

Cargill glared at his tormentor. "You had your chance. If you didn't find them it is not my fault."

Trout furiously threw his right fist into the pit of Cargill's stomach. The victim tightened his abdominals with all his might to receive the blow, creating a dull thud as the punch landed. Trout's knuckles felt like he had punched a brick wall. Angrily, he resumed pounding on the stomach from left and right, viciously trying to knock the air out of the man, but Richard Cargill greeted each blow with masculine grunts and groans of ooghs and ughs.

Now Trout turned and shouted an order to the warriors, as Cargill gasped for air in an attempt to recover from his beating. Struggling to breathe, he flexed arms and legs, lifting his torso until his arms were parallel with the log. After frantically inhaling precious oxygen for several seconds, he slowly lowered his body to resume its crucifixion stretching.

The females were taken aback by this display. They seemed to be mesmerized by the strength and defiance shown to them by the prisoner, but Trout repeated his order to Blue-face, who jolted the warriors into action. They immediately ran for the storage hut, where they each retrieved a five-foot pole one inch in diameter, then returned to the crucified man to form a circle of 12 around him.

Trout looked up to his victim. "This is your last chance, doctor. Where are my diamonds?"

Cargill flexed his chest in defiance. "Go to hell."

Leaning down to grab the lower log, he began spinning the prisoner and twisting the ropes above together. Soon two became one and Trout gave the victim a shove. Cargill swung towards the edge of the circle, where he was greeted by the rounded end of a pole. He grunted as the pole jabbed into the middle of his back to break the swinging momentum.

Using her pole to push, that warrior then sent Cargill in another direction, only to be greeted by another jab into his gut. The helpless man was sent from one part of the circle to another, and all the while, the ropes were unwinding and spinning him in a clockwise direction.

Cargill grunted with each attack, as he was mercilessly jabbed by one wooden pole after another. His swinging motion only increased the weight of the rocks at his feet and worsened his stretching.

Like a human pendulum, Richard Cargill was randomly poked and jabbed again and again until the ropes were completely unwound. Changing the angle of their weapons, the savages now whacked Cargill's crucified torso with the sides of their poles when he swung in their direction. The wooden weapons now being used like whips, Cargill's skin stung with each smack on his stretched body. The momentum of his swinging gradually decreased, making the diameter of circles take him out of reach of the tormenting poles. The warriors stood their ground silently, as the beaten man swung in smaller and smaller circles, finally becoming stationary in the center of the perimeter.

Cargill was groaning in agony. Small red spots and long red lines dotted his skin on the back, chest, stomach and buttocks. The stretching and crucifixion were taking their toll, causing his breath to become more labored.

"How do you feel now?" asked Trout. "Are you ready to talk?"

With the need for oxygen critical, Cargill summoned his strength and flexed every muscle to pull his body up and alleviate the pressure. The she-warriors gasped at this manly display, but Trout was not impressed. He launched another assault on the tightened abdominal muscles.

"Damn you, come back down here. Do you think you can defy me? I will break you, doctor. Talk now!"

The powerful man jutted out his lower jaw to answer between each punch. "You... will... never... break me."

And with that, Cargill slowly allowed his body to return to its stretching. Trout took the opportunity to land his punches to the prisoner's chest and rib cage. Now he was crimson with anger, but soon tired of throwing punches to the man's defenseless torso.

The tormentor nodded to Blue-face. She barked an order and the 12 warriors left the circle. Passing their poles to the next group, a new circle of 12 was formed. Two at a time they ran towards the helpless man. Simultaneously,

Cargill was speared on opposite sides of his stretched body by the poles.

The first of these dual assaults was launched in the middle of his back coupled with the sternum. The poles were driven into him like stakes, bringing pressure to his chest and back at the same time. Cargill gasped in shock from the initial blow, then emitted manly groans as the warriors stood their ground to drive their poles into him like daggers. Meanwhile, Trout stood by to continue the questioning.

"Where are my diamonds, Cargill? Where did you hide them?"

The crucified man continued with his tortured grunts, summoning all of his strength to withstand the poles grinding into him. Blue-face shouted a command and the two removed their weapons, exiting the circled perimeter as two more immediately charged towards him from opposite sides. One pole struck Cargill's lower back, while the other was embedded into his stomach. He flexed and writhed, expanding his chest and sucking in his abdominal cavity best he could.

The savage females in waiting beyond the perimeter were all smiles and giggles, relishing in the poor man's suffering, as Trout continued to torment his prisoner.

"Talk Cargill. Talk now. You have lost. Talk and I will make them stop."

Cargill, oblivious to the questioning, shut tight his eyes and focused his mind on withstanding this devastating assault on his abdomen and lower spine. The pressure upon him intense, he thought they intended to run him though, but just when he thought he could take no more, Blue-face ordered two to leave and two to replace them. Poles now were driven into the man's rib cage, one on each side, forced towards each other with Cargill caught in between. He howled from the agony of unrelenting pressure grinding into his exposed ribs, every muscle flexed to capacity.

Each spearing pair of savage warriors were allowed two minuted to torture their crucified victim, each pair targeting any part of him from belly to arm pits. He groaned and grunted with each new assault, while Trout relentlessly tried to coax the answer from him, until finally, Cargill had withstood 10 attacks and only two warriors were left. Trout turned from the prisoner and spoke softly to Blue-face, and soon a warrior brought Trout a stool of two-feet height which he placed to Cargill's side. He stepped up to meet his victim face-to-cheek.

"Have you had enough? You must talk."

Cargill lifted his head, moaning from the agony inflicted upon him. "You will never break me."

"Oh, you think not? Wait until you feel this."

Blue-face directed the two remaining warriors and they walked towards the prisoner. As one placed her pole just above his tail bone, the other put her pole just above the center of his pelvic bone. Then they slowly started pushing towards each other. Cargill writhied as the front pole ground into the lowest part of his abdomen. Shockwaves reverberated from his belly into his groin, and when he tried to raise his legs to alleviate this ungodly pressure, Blue-face sadistically put her foot onto the log to keep him stretched. With all the strength they could muster, two female savages ground their poles into him with devastating ferocity.

"Talk doctor. Give me my diamonds."

He could not talk. All he could do was make sounds as though he were about to puke. Richard Cargill was about to puke, but with bile lining his throat, teeth gritting and groin burning, he gurgled a defiant response. "I will never tell you."

"Your answers have already given you up, Cargill. What you say tells me you know where they are. It is all over. Tell me."

Trout babbled on non-stop, but Richard Cargill did not hear him. He threw back his head and looked to the heavens. This simultaneous attack on his coccyx and belly, combined with his torturous crucifixion pushed him to the brink. With a mighty groan, his body collapsed and he lost consciousness.

Trout ordered all torture to stop and poles removed, fearful he had pushed his prisoner over the edge before getting his answer. He shouted for a bowl of water, and after wetting his hand he desperately tried to revive his prisoner, dabbing the liquid on Cargill's forehead and cheeks, lightly tapping and hoping for a response. He could hear and see the man's labored breathing, and he ordered the warriors to remove the lower log.

As the straps were cut from his ankles, Cargill groggily lifted his head, sighing with relief as his stretching was lessened. Trout offered him the bowl of water and the tortured man eagerly drank. Revived, Cargill flexed his chest and arms to lift his torso higher. Drenched in sweat, his body glimmering in the heated air of dusk, shards of sunlight filtering through treetops surrounding the village, Cargill posed in all his masculine glory. Every line and curve of muscle was clearly highlighted by sweat and exertion, as he defied gravity to raise himself, to suck in air. In awe of him, the she-warriors did not quite understanding how this powerful man could possibly withstand their tortures. Despite all they had inflicted upon him, he still found the strength to display himself before them, to mock them, and to perhaps entice them.

After several deep breaths of chest-expanding oxygen, Cargill allowed gravity to resume his crucifixion, and although Trout was relieved by his prisoner's recovery, he still had but one purpose in mind. "Why don't you talk, Dr. Cargill? Nobody wants to see you suffer like this."

"You are worse than these savages, Trout. At least you know what you are doing is wrong. I pity them, but I despise you."

"Soon I will be forced to give you up to these savages. We will see how much you pity them after they have finished with you. Unlike me, they will show no mercy. I suspect that soon you will be begging for me to help you, to make them stop torturing you. Then you will tell me everything."

Part 4 - The Milking Tree

Roger Trout stepped down from his stool and transferred control to Blue-face. She summoned several females to follow her while the rest sat on the ground admiring their naked prisoner, and when they returned Blue-face was carrying a bowl, four warriors were carrying two buckets apiece, and several others came with jungle undergrowth that they threw into the pit. Hot coals reignited to flame, illuminating the center of the village clearing. Night had come. The naked form of Dr. Richard Cargill hanging in suspended crucifixion was bathed in a heated glow of orange. His sweat sparkled.

As Blue-face drifted towards the pit four female Natashi placed their buckets near Cargill's feet.

Trout hovered nearby and spoke. "Dr. Cargill, aren't you curious as to how I came to be here?"

"I suppose you'll tell me whether I want to hear it or not."

"I'm glad you asked. My expedition never made it out of this jungle. The

Natashi took us all prisoner and brought us here to be executed like you saw today."

As the man was speaking, he motioned to the warriors behind him. "I knew it was the Natashi as soon as I heard their spine-chilling calls in the jungle. I had read about them in old journals from early Dutch explorers."

Cargill was distracted by the activities of the women. Two of them stood at his feet and were rubbing some sort of white colored liquid on his legs, feet and ankles. "What the hell are they doing?"

"Oh, never mind that. I'm sure you have read about this tribe, their fierce nature, their savage treatment of men. Well, I immediately knew there was only one way for me to survive. That was to sacrifice my men to appease these savage women."

Two more females now mounted two-foot stools and were applying the thick, milky substance to Cargill's chest, belly, arms and backside. The manner of the application became an erotic body rub, causing Cargill to sense feelings of arousal, but he diverted his attention to hold back these reactions. "What is this crap they're smearing on me?"

"I'll tell you in time. Now, pay attention. I gave up all 30 of my men and then, about every 10 days I would watch one of them be ritualistically tortured and executed, just as you saw today. Their leader forced me to extract the men's sperm and vomit on their tree. Again, this kept me alive. I became quite proficient at sucking dicks, only so I could get it over with as quickly as possible."

Cargill was now fascinated by the story, but still worried about the female activity all around him. "Please tell me what they're doing."

"Damn it, forget about that for now. This is important." Trout was determined to somehow justify his actions of the last 16 years. "Not only did I give them my men, I promised them many more. I told them of the trade routes 300 miles north of here. Once every six months, 12 Natashi and I would journey there. At night we would sneak into camps, taking two or three male captives and bringing them back here for slaughter. We could have taken as many as we wanted, but I figured this number would be the most we should take without attracting too much attention. So that is how I survived all these years. I knew there was no escape. I had to stay until either they killed me or someone like you came along looking for my treasure. You answered my every prayer."

Trout seemed relieved that he had finally been able to tell his story, hoping the prisoner would somehow understand and perhaps forgive.

Now Cargill's body was encased with the white goo. All that was left to cover were his face and genitals. The substance slowly started to sting and burn his skin, already sensitive from the relentless beatings. "What is this gunk? It burns. Tell me what the hell it is."

"Dr. Cargill, you are suspended under the Natashi Milking Tree. This is their god. One time per year a man is chosen to be subjected to a test of endurance under their tree. You, my unfortunate friend, have been chosen. I can probably stop this from happening, but you must talk to me. You know the question."

"You are sick. What happened to you? You were once respected the world over. Now you're just a sadistic maniac."

"It is called survival, doctor. I suggest you start learning to adapt. Do you know what these women really want? Penises. They worship the male penis. The man himself is useless to them, but their manly organs are sacred."

As the women applied the substance to Cargill's face, he gazed down to see that Blue-face had returned from the pit. Standing before the crucified man, she reached into the bowl to present a human penis. She had cooked it in the pit, and she held the charred organ high into the air. Looking up to the branches of The Milking Tree, Blue-face recited some sort of chant, perhaps a prayer, and then stuffed the cooked phallus into her mouth, swallowing it whole.

Cargill recoiled in horror at this macabre spectacle. As the other she-warriors mimicked her chant, Blue-face reached into the bowl, producing a second penis. Cargill turned away when the savage again forced the organ down her throat.

Suddenly, Cargill realized that the effects of the paste were changing. As the goo began to dry and thicken, the burning sensations were replaced by feelings of manliness. The chemicals, or drugs or whatever was in the goop, caused his nuts to send testosterone throughout his bloodstream, and his cock received plenty of this blood as well.

Meanwhile, Blue-face presented the third penis to the night sky, confirming for Cargill what he already knew. This female savage had indeed severed his poor men's masculinity, had separated their cocks from them before their battered carcasses were thrown into the fire. And all because of a fucking tree.

The outrage he felt was indescribable, as he watched her swallow for the third time, but his outrage was soon overtaken by the incredible sensations reverberating throughout his body. His dick was now fully erect. Blue-face reached into the nearby bucket, and then plastered his genitals with the tantalizing paste. First she encased Cargill's dangling testicles. Next came the phallus. She spread erotic substance over the entire length of his engorged penis, lingering there with her taunting fingers, slowly stroking back and forth on the shaft of the organ. And all the while, Blue-face smiled at him, not a smile of kindness, but of sadistic lust, lust to inflict more punishment upon him, lust to incorporate his manly, nine-inch-long and two-inch-thick cock with her tortures. Her brightly white teeth grinned an evil grin. Blue-face would prove beyond doubt that hers was the superior gender.

Cargill was overwhelmed by the sense of helplessness, of humiliation and vulnerability. He arched his back and thrust his pelvis forward hoping to startle her into releasing his cock, but to no avail. She held his hardened penis in her hand and squeezed tightly, continuing to mock him with her blue lines centered by flashing teeth.

He gazed at his audience. Every female scrutinized his masculine form in bondage, his Caucasian skin covered in chalky white. They marveled at his impressive tool, whispering and pointing and giggling. He dreaded the thought of losing his cock. What man doesn't? He shuddered to envision its being severed from his body, revulsed by the image whether his body was alive or dead, and he pleaded with Roger Trout, "Make them stop. What are they doing to me?"

Trout nodded to Blue-face and she released her taunting grip on Cargill's manhood.

"Dr. Cargill, I have watched this ritual for 16 years. No man has ever survived their test of endurance. And when the man fails, their treatment of him becomes brutal beyond words. I cannot begin to count the many different ways I've seen men tortured. Don't let it happen to you. Talk to me now. Quickly."

"We will both die here. After they kill me, who will be left for them to butcher but you? They certainly won't kill their own. Your time will come."

"I am aware of this, my friend. It saddens me that you have chosen this path. I wish you well."

Trout left the circle and turned the prisoner over to the women. They had now surrounded the suspended man. 12 females stood on their two-foot stools encircling him. Cargill's manly body writhed and undulated from the erotic sensations pulsating throughout. He again struggled to breathe, and so he flexed his muscles, pulling himself up for several quick gasps of air, a momentary relief from the stretching. Enraptured by this display of masculinity, every female present gasped wide-eyed, for now not only did his powerful muscles hypnotize them, so to did his awe-inspiring fuck tool. Cargill's cock pierced the air like a spear in flight, thick, juicy and intimidating. With the paste thickening, its effect unleashed new rounds of testosterone inside him, which caused his scrotum to involuntarily clinch, which caused his mighty cock to spring towards his belly. Repeatedly,

Cargill's thick and elongated worm waved up and down to them, as he slowly lowered his body and resumed the crucified posture of an heroic, defiant, sex-starved man.

He experienced sensations never before known to him. This ecstasy was higher than foreplay, higher than post-orgasm and yes, perhaps even higher than orgasm itself. His erect cock tried to expand well beyond its nine inches, if only its skin would allow it. His body writhed, belly sucked in, chest thrust forward, cock thrust forward, as he physically begged for them to ravish him. Females were tempted. These savages were being driven to madness from the sight of this amazing, mysterious white man. His powerful penis throbbed before them. His glorious muscles flexed, highlighted by the milky paste, fire from the nearby pit increasing his glow.

Cargill again pulled himself up until his shoulders touched the log, but this time it was not to breathe. He arched his back as though performing a swan dive, inviting the females to come to him, to engulf him with their salivating mouths and pussy holes. His protruding cock contracted and bobbed upwards with each heartbeat, the gooey white substance mixing with pre-come and oozing a long silky strand from his slit to the ground below.

She-warriors on either side of Cargill had the most tantalizing view, as he flexed his muscles to maintain this pull-up position. They could follow the manly line of his body starting from his rugged jaw jutting out, then curving back to the adam's apple. Flexed arms deepened his pits, thick hair matted by the erotic paste. Suddenly, the line protrudes forward, defining his powerful chest flexing and straining against gravity, two tiny tips of his tits emerging from the paste. Next came a dramatic curve inward under his rib cage, flowing down the length of his flexed and flattened belly, only to be gloriously interrupted by his pulsating, mighty phallus penetrating the air, begging for something more meaningful to fuck.

This all-encompassing display of manliness brought moans from his female spectators. Anticipation drove them to madness, as they marked time on their stools as though they had to pee. They frantically massaged their vaginas as salivating juices ran down their ebony legs.

Blue-face circled behind the man and launched him. He swung towards the circle's perimeter, where the chosen female reached out for a crucified, hard-dicked man. As his swinging body reached her, she clamped her hands onto his buttocks and inserted his magnificent penis into her pussy hole. She pressed his pelvis against hers and forced his manly organ deep into her vaginal walls, burying him into the heavenly surroundings of her pulsating clitoris. High-pitched shrieks were matched by deep-toned and manly groans, as she began to thrust her pelvis forward and back, riding this magnificent mount.

Cargill's belly and cock were pulled forward, while the crucifixion log pulled his arms back. He flexed his arms and expanded his chest, further displaying his manliness. His legs hung hanging limp towards the ground, toes frantically curled forward, and then arched back. This pose created a scene of heroic sacrifice. Cargill offered up his manly tool for her to do with as she pleased. And what she pleased to do was clutch her fingertips into his buttocks, thrusting his powerful unit deep inside her.

The upward angle of his approach maximized the stimulation of her clitoris, his swollen mushroom head perfectly shaped to make contact. Convulsions reverberated throughout her body as she frantically pounded his enlarged organ into her. Cargill gazed down his expanded chest to watch her work him over. He could feel her rounded breasts bouncing against him, her erect nipples driving under his rib cage again and again. His own nipples became stimulated, their tips erect and protruding out of the erotic paste. Their orgasms were conjoined in time. Sounds never before heard reverberated throughout the village. Wild beasts in the surrounding jungle awoke and alerted themselves to danger. Birds took to the wing from what they did not know.

The she-warrior kept him inside her until she could take no more. She released him to return to the center of the circle, while she collapsed to the ground, arching her back and thrusting her nipples toward the branches of The Milking Tree. The incredible power of this man continued to pulsate inside her long after his penis had been released.

Soon he was again in his stationary position, hanging crucified in the center of the circle, his cock still throbbing and ready for more. Blue-face sent him on his way. A second pair of hands clasped onto his buttocks and his incredible cock thrust inside a female warrior. Both man and woman cried out from the incredible sensations, as the spectacle was repeated. Soon he shot his mighty load into her, knocking her off her pedestal to writhe under the tree.

And so it continued. One after another, the fierce female warriors fell like bowling pins to the ground, fucked by a he-man, rendered useless rags to convulse, to thrust their nipples to the sky. The power of this mysterious man consumed the entire tribe - and one outsider.

Midway through the ordeal, Cargill's mind and body were tiring. He knew the paste would keep him erect as long as he could focus on the task at hand, but maintaining this focus was becoming more difficult for him. Thus, the test of which Trout had spoken.

Using the atmosphere of the jungle around him, Cargill instigated an animalistic aggression as a way to motivate himself. He re-invigorated his resolve with expressions of his masculine superiority. He taunted the inferior women, knowing they couldn't understand his language anyhow.

Each time a warrior took him into her, Cargill flexed his arms and bulged his chest to capacity. He grunted, gorilla-like, mocked her, dominatingly glared at her and challenged her. "You will never defeat me. I am too much man for all of you. I will service you and the next and the next until all of you have had enough. I will fuck all of you to oblivion. I will survive your goddamned test."

Interspersed with this language were animal sounds, grunts and ughs.

Cargill spoke the language of lust-crazed sex. That's all the Natashi needed to hear. It's universal. The combination of his powerful cock battering one clitoris after another, coupled with his animalistic verbal, facial and bodily expressions brought each of them to orgasm before they even knew what hit them. And Dr. Richard Cargill, crucified he-man, was there for them each and every time, maintaining his massive erection and pumping one manly load after another into savage female pussies.

Trout heard every word. He watched with amazement, as Cargill rendered one she-warrior after another into convulsing rags, writhing under the sacred Milking Tree. Trout himself was consumed by this man, and his infatuation caused his own pecker to bulge out from beneath his loin wrapping. He tired of trying to keep it concealed and removed the wrapping, along with his ridiculous vegetation crown, joining the rest of the tribe in naked glory.

Finally, there was but one of the twelve Natashi left unserviced. Cargill's body hung limp in the center of the circle. The only movement came from his rapid breath and still bobbing, erect penis. Lying on the ground, 11 females dreamily gazed at the night sky through the branches of The Milking Tree, still mesmerized by their prisoner's incredible masculinity. Vaginas continued to pulsate, vibrating from the aftershocks left behind by this man's amazing organ.

The lone female awaited his cock. Self-induced orgasm could have come to her long ago, as she patiently watched the 11 before her serviced by this glorious man, but she had restrained herself. Now her reward was at hand. He had already surpassed the performance of any others in the known history of the tribe. She was the chosen one, the Natashi female warrior prepared and honored to take this man to his triumph.

Blue-face sent him to her and their contact was instant ecstasy. Again the man's penis was engulfed by pulsating vaginal walls. She squeezed him with all her might, crushing his manly tool inside her. She waited patiently for him. Longing for this since his ordeal began, she now would take his magnificent penis to new heights, coaxing him to shoot.

She thrust herself back and forth, squeezing her powerful vaginal muscles around him. His dick felt as though she were standing on him barefooted, and he relished it. She prodded him, she worshipped him and manhandled him until he was ready. His mighty chest bulged as he prepared to shoot the final manly load.

Again, savage animal sounds permeated the village, as simultaneous orgasms brought two lovers to the pinnacles of ecstasy. She crushed his cock deep inside her, savagely coaxing out every ounce of manly come he had left to offer. He growled in ecstatic pleasure and pain, as she tortured his cock long after his orgasm was finished and seed extracted.

Then, mercifully, she released him back to the tribal leader and collapsed to the ground, joining the eleven before her who had partaken of this incredible man.

Now the entire tribe moved towards Cargill as he hung limp under the magical tree. They surrounded and knelt before him in reverence and awe. Those who had not felt his power reached out to touch him, to be a part of this historic moment, but Blue-face ordered them out of the circle. She was not yet convinced. Having not yet experienced his power, she now isolated and prepared him for his final ordeal. He still had not offered his sacrifice to the Natashi god, The Milking Tree.

Part 5 - Consecration

Cargill was completely exhausted. He had been bound in suspended crucifixion for hours. His body had been beaten, poked and drained of manly sperm again and again. The enormous amount of sweat he had produced was beginning to dissolve the stimulating paste and allow his erection to fade.

In the background stood Roger Trout. He had fully intended to continue the interrogation after Cargill failed the endurance test, but the man had not failed. His amazing performance had subdued the savage females and Trout himself was been more than impressed by the man's virility. More than that, he was totally overwhelmed by the power and manly strength, and now it was his responsibility to extract and provide this man's seed for sacrifice to the tree. Beyond that, Trout was consumed by his own personal urges to become part of this amazing man. His own penis throbbed as he entered the circle and approached Cargill.

Blue-face intercepted him, stopping him dead in his tracks. She ordered Trout out of the circle, making it clear to him that she would be the one to perform this sacred duty. Trout obediently stepped aside. He no longer felt threatened by the Natashi warriors or Blue-face. He wanted to be part of this glorious ritual, which had already reached historic proportions, and so he joined the female warriors sitting on the ground under The Milking Tree to absorb the incredible masculinity displayed above them. All were enraptured.

Kneeling before the tortured man, Blue-face took his fading penis into her mouth. Cargill twitched from this attack, jolted out of his dream state to the realization that his ordeal was not yet over. His mind, however, stirred to defiance. With the paste having lost its effect, Cargill knew that only will power could save him. After all he had been through, he was not about to let Blue-face win this battle, execute him and sadistically sever his cock. Of course, unbeknownst to him, Cargill no longer lived with this threat. He could never guess that it no longer existed, because the Natashi now worshipped him as a kind of man-god. Oblivious, Cargill focused every thought to one goal, and that was to shoot into this savage's mouth and prove to her that, as a man, he was her equal.

Between his will-power and her oral worship, the erection was achieved. Cargill's self-motivating animal lust now returned, stimulating himself to perform for her.

"Tonight you've seen a real man in action. So, you want some, too. Is that it? You can have it. None of your tortures will defeat me. I am more than you can deal with, you savage. I will choke you when I shoot my load."

Trout had to restrain himself when he heard Cargill's motivational speech. What kind of man was this? How could anyone service so many and still be prepared to give more? He clasped his hands behind his back to keep from jacking himself off, as one touch of his penis would cause him to explode.

As Trout struggled, Blue-face took control of Cargill. For hours she'd watched the evening's festivities with skepticism, but as this man had answered every beating and challenge one by one, she also became enraptured by this man's power. And now the focus of his strength was right where she wanted it to be: buried inside her mouth.

How long had she and her people waited for such a man to come to them? What an incredible honor she had been given. Here was the only man in the history of the Natashi tribe to pass the test of The Milking Tree, and she was the one to sacrifice this greatest gift to their god. This overwhelming honor fueled her passion to give this incredible man the performance of her life. This was not any kind of oral service, but something divine, a gift from the gods themselves.

Cargill sensed the excitement coming from the mouth of Blue-face. Her intense praise of him reverberated from his dick to his head to his toes. He flexed his arms and pulled his shoulders up to the log, forcing Blue-face to follow him upwards in order to continue her oral worship.

The spectators gasped at this amazing display of strength. They could see his mighty chest and powerful belly flexed to capacity, his manly grunts and verbal taunts driving them to madness. One of the she-warriors lost all control and pounced upon Trout, inserting his hardened pecker into her. Others now joined in, as they pinned his arms and legs spread eagled onto the ground. All the females who had not been fortunate enough to partake of Cargill now used Trout to fulfill their desires. Roger Trout was up to the task. As long as he was able to see the magnificent crucified Cargill being serviced by the Natashi leader, Trout could perform for them. And perform he did.

Cargill was mesmerized by the scene on the ground before him. Coupling this scene of orgy with memories of his own glorious orgasms, he could now see that two incredible displays of masculinity were simultaneously subduing the fierce Natashi warriors. As he watched the man below thoroughly satisfy one lust-crazed female after another, Cargill knew that both he and Trout had been elevated to the status of god.

This startling realization overwhelmed him and he easily summoned a huge load of sperm, flooding it into Blue-face. The incredible velocity of the explosion nearly choked her, but she was sworn to carry out her sacred duty and recovered to consume every last drop of his manly come.

Now she released the organ and rose to her feet, signaling to the rest of the tribe that it was time. They stopped their activities and drifted towards the symbol of Natashi power. Raising her hands to the sky, Blue-face gave praise to the mighty Milking Tree.

Roger Trout rose to his feet, his dick fully erect, and followed them towards the tree. Stopping before the crucified man, he looked up and smiled.

Cargill smiled in return. "There it is my friend, it is yours."

Trout immediately knelt and took the half-hard organ into his mouth. Finally, it was his turn. He abandoned all notions of the sacred ritual. How many dicks had he been forced to suck so he could spit sperm onto a friggin' tree? This was what he had waited for - 16 years of waiting. A real man. A man whose sperm meant something.

His enthusiastic assault immediately brought Cargill to full erection. The man's powerful penis once again throbbed as it was lovingly worshipped. Trout took his moistened lips to the base of the unit, forcing the bulging head deep into his throat. He held it there and squeezed with all his might, pressing with his tongue and roof of mouth.

Cargill flexed and groaned at this incredible sensation. Now Trout slowly drew back his lips, gently massaging the underside of the shaft with his tongue, as he approached the head. Once there, his tongue lovingly wrapped around the underside, further stimulating the throbbing mushroom. Cargill twitched his fingers and toes. The incredible oral worship was driving him to madness. He had serviced 13 females, but the sensational praise lavished on his penis by this man was beyond heaven.

Blue-face performed the sacrifice, gagging herself and regurgitating the powerful man's sperm onto the trunk. Then, she gently placed her lips onto the tree and consecrated the sacred fluid with a gentle kiss, forever uniting this incredible masculinity with her Natashi tribe.

Blue-face began a woeful song of praise. For the first time, her gentle, feminine voice was heard.

This enchanting sound soothed Cargill. The pure beauty of it nearly brought him to tears and he gazed down his racked body to see Trout kneeling before him, heaping his praise upon his tireless cock.

The expertise, the slavish worship, the incredible heights of ecstasy were more than any man could deserve. The love he felt for everyone in the village consumed him, as he absorbed the realization that he had conquered and subdued this tribe of females with his incredible masculinity. The Natashi women had found a new respect and admiration for the male gender, thanks to these two men.

Trout's incredible expertise finished him and he shot another manly load into the eager mouth below. This time the orgasm was not one of lust, but of admiration and respect for all those who had serviced him this night. The emotion overwhelmed him and he cried out, as Trout continued to coax the last drops of precious fluid from his he-man.

The entire tribe now encircled Cargill and he was released from his suspension. The ropes were lowered and log cut from his wrists. He was laid spread eagled on the ground and surrounded by the tribe, including Blueface and Roger Trout. They began dribbling him with spit and washing away the remnants of erotic paste. Cargill basked in this worship, as they lovingly massaged his tormented body, working their saliva deep into his muscles and every crevice from his armpits to the skin between his toes .

Sacrifice made and released from bondage, Richard Cargill was comforted and lavished with praise. The Milking Tree festivities were soon ended and all the Natashi drifted to their huts, dreamily enchanted by the magical evening they had experienced.

Fem Fist Books

Part 6 - Two Worlds are One

Cargill and Trout were escorted to the grand hut, the residence of Blue-face. There, Cargill was attended to by his two admirers. They fed him, bathed him and treated his skin with moisturizing ointments.

For three days and nights, Cargill, Trout and Blue-face were seen by no one. During the nights, nobody in the village slept. They laid awake on their floor mats absorbing the animal sounds emanating from the grand hut, and because these sounds reminded the females of what they'd felt when the cock of Richard Cargill overwhelmed them, they summoned the men of their tribe from their dwelling. Their ankle bindings were cut and they were taken to the second-most important and largest hut of the village, where the six eldest Natashi females lived. Here, the three men were shown the art of making love like real men, not as slaves. No longer were they subjugated to mere functional intercourse, but instead were taken to utopia, absorbed into the new-found enlightenment of the Natashi females.

The three inhabitants of the grand hut worshipped one another, constantly changing combinations to please each other two on one. Blue-face was fulfilled countless times. Triangles were formed. Lips, fingers and tongues massaged and stimulated, bringing untold orgasms to each of them. The three lovers from two different worlds melded all their morals and desires together, radically changing both worlds forever.

When Cargill finally emerged from the hut, he stretched his naked body in all its glory to greet the morning sun. Blue-face and Trout remained inside on the sleeping mat, both of them chest down with his left arm draped over her shoulder and her right arm draped over his. Saturating the ground beneath the mat, the flow of their still-warm blood, once gushers, now trickled from their freshly-cut throats. And one by one Cargill visited Natashi huts, insisting that fierce Natashi females accept his cock into their pussy holes from behind while on their hands and knees, so that he could stifle their screams with his cupped hand as he slit their throats.

An arduous task it was, but Cargill thoroughly enjoyed each fuck. Methodically and magically he reduced their numbers, and when he finally entered what was now the orgy hut where three tribal men were busy poking into and being molested by six tribal women, Richard Cargill was confronted with a rather difficult decision.

What should he do with the three Natashi men? He certainly couldn't kill them, too. They'd done nothing but suffer themselves since the day they were born. And what of the six remaining Natashi women? Did his rage and desire to exact revenge justify the obliteration of an entire people? No, it did not, and besides, neither the female warriors nor their male lovers even noticed him standing there with bloody hand holding bloody blade. Nine serpentine forms of glistening ebony skin writhed, undulated and intermingled in a ceaseless festival of unbridled sex, a new method of entertainment, and all of it because he, Dr. Richard Cargill, had satisfied the challenge of their Milking Tree.

Although he was tempted to join them, Cargill had other priorities. In the Blue-face hut were his western clothes, his charts, his notes, and the Kutambi Elephant. He made preparations for his return to civilization. Once dressed and supplied with provisions of food and water, Cargill approached the pit, stoked its embers with a branch taken from The Milking Tree and gathered flame onto the branch. He set all reachable canopy afire. No more Milking Tree, no more need for sadistic rituals of regurgitated sperm and severed cocks, and as flame from one branch jumped to another and another, Dr. Richard Cargill left this village to its own fate. At the pace those three men and six women were going at it inside their hut, oblivious to Cargill while they fornicated a mile a minute, he expected they'd have the village repopulated in no time.

His tusks were intact, still wrapped in a pair of his cargo shorts and right where he'd buried them. Reaching the edge of Natashi jungle, Cargill was greeted by a vast plain. One hundred miles stood between him and civilization, but he made it, urged on by motivational speeches not far removed from those used underneath The Milking Tree.

"Torture me, will ya? Crucify me? Beat me? HA! Crazy bitches. Didn't know what they were dealing with. Milk my cock, huh? Think you're going to take it from me? Fat chance, woman. Fuck 'em... fuck 'em all... that's what I did."

Back home, Cargill had the statue and tusks expertly mended together. At auction, he watched in amazement as the bids for his Kutambi Elephant climbed higher and higher, far surpassing the estimated value of his hard-earned treasure. A fitting end to his wild adventure, he thought, and even though he enjoyed slitting the throats of that crazed cock sucker, Roger Trout, and his sadistic female Natashi partner, Blue-face, counting his millions was Cargill's ultimate revenge against all who participated in his tortures.

The next several years were devoted to one singular goal: duplicating that erotic paste. He paid a staff of chemists vast sums of cash in his efforts. He hired countless escorts and set up countless orgies to test what his chemists put together, but none of them ever quite got it right. In the end, it didn't matter. Richard Cargill came to the realization that his brain was all he needed. His memories of that magical evening transformed him from a sophisticated, well-traveled man, to a beastly, come-spewing masterpiece.

After installing his own Milking Tree in his own mansion, word of his parties spread like wildfire. Females from the world over paid him for the privelege of torturing him. "Go ahead, woman. Do your worst!" he'd grunt while hanging crucified and naked and waving his hard-as-stone nine-inch cock. Doing their worst resulted in them writhing on the floor, thrusting their tits towards the night time sky separated by a two-story solarium. And why wouldn't they? What possible threat could they pose for him? Richard Cargill conquered an entire tribe of fierce, female warriors with that cock of his. He feared no woman.

The mighty phallus is a powerful force, and that is exactly why no man should fear anyone at anytime anywhere.

Holy fucking crap! Ain't men beautiful?

Go Ahead, Woman. Do Your Worst!

Fem Fist Books

Go Ahead, Woman. Do Your Worst!

About the Author
Jasper McCutcheon

You might know Jasper from his audio series, Uncle Jasper's Five-fingered Bedtime Stories, available as Podcasts or downloadable as audio MP3's from his nephew's web site, Jardonn's Erotic Tales.com. Jasper's tales, both audio and written are derived from the many people he has met through the years, working-class nobodies like himself who strive to get by month to month while enjoying life to its fullest.

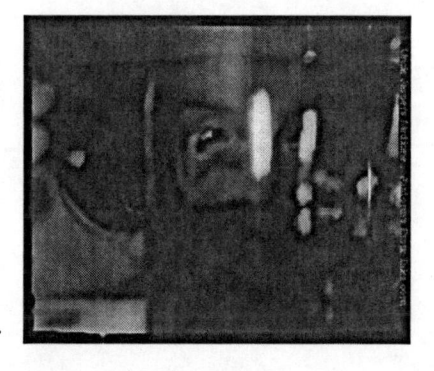

Jasper McCutcheon is also the author of:

Maggie Pie (Nazca Plains, 2007)

I Was Tortured By the Pygmy Love Queen (2007)

Available at Goodboner.com, Jardonnserotictales.com or your local bookstore.